MW01138661

A SEAL's Surrender

AN ALPHA SEALS NOVEL

Makenna Jameison

ISBN: 9781717911377

Table of Contents

Chapter 1

Lexi Mattingly flipped her sleek, jet black hair over her shoulder and strode through the parking lot, her sky-high heels clicking as she walked across the black asphalt. The sweltering heat hit her like a sauna, the salty air that was blowing in from the ocean the only thing making it somewhat tolerable. She slipped off her suit jacket, walking the remaining few steps to her SUV in only her slim skirt and camisole.

The vast spread of buildings around Naval Amphibious Base Little Creek was nothing like the impenetrable rings of corridors at the Pentagon, her home turf. The only thing vaguely familiar was the sounds of planes in the air—although the fighter jets screaming across the sky on training drills from Oceana Naval Air Station in Virginia Beach weren't exactly the same as the commercial flights taking off from Reagan National Airport along the Potomac River in Arlington.

She watched two FA-18 Hornets blaze across the blue sky, the image reminding her of a lifetime ago in Coronado. It was hard to believe nearly ten years had gone by since her days as a college student back in California. She'd built her career in Washington, DC, her drive to succeed and work ethic fitting in perfectly with the fast-paced, challenging lifestyle of the Department of Defense.

An IT whiz at the Pentagon, amongst the Defense Department's best-of-the-best, Lexi was called down to Little Creek to determine who was attempting to hack into the Top Secret databases at the naval base. Black Ops, names and identities of SEAL teams, mission specs, locations of forward-operating bases around the world—the intelligence stored there would be a wealth of information to foreign operatives. It would fetch a high price on the black market and make the US vulnerable to foreign adversaries. Lexi was tasked to ensure that the data never fell into the wrong hands. And to determine the source of the attempted infiltrations.

After spending the afternoon briefing the top brass at Little Creek about the vulnerabilities of their computer systems, she was ready to call it a day. Four hours of bumper-to-bumper traffic on I-95 and I-64 as she drove down from Arlington this morning followed by four hours spent in a cramped conference room on base, and she needed a drink. Preferably a stiff one.

She slung her suit jacket over one arm and clicked the remote to unlock her vehicle. The *chirp, chirp* resounded across the pavement. She certainly didn't need to set the alarm while on base, but old habits died hard.

A uniformed Navy officer eyed her appreciatively as he climbed out of his own car a few spaces over, but he merely nodded with a polite, "Ma'am."

She nodded back in acknowledgement and then smirked as she turned away. All the military men were so formal on base, under the watchful eyes of their supervisors and commanding officers. Get them in a bar after hours, a few drinks in, and they'd be hitting on her left and right. Insisting she needed to come home with them for the night.

Right.

She could also use a month-long vacation to a tropical island, but the chance of either of those things happening was zilch.

She hadn't minded the attention of handsome military men in the least in her college days. Back in California, hunky guys, hot beaches, and alcohol-fueled nights had filled her early twenties. Her first and only serious boyfriend, a ruggedly handsome Navy SEAL, had kept her up night after night, and she'd been more than happy to lose sleep basking in his attention. To let his years of experience guide her first sexual encounters. They were young, carefree, and had the world at their disposal.

Those days were long over now.

At twenty-nine, she'd spent the past seven years working her way up the ranks at the Department of Defense. She had an undergraduate degree in Computer Science, a Master's Degree from Georgetown that she'd completed while working full time—and she was good at what she did. Really good. An expert hacker and IT Security Specialist for the Pentagon. Her expertise and vast knowledge was renowned, sought after by others in the military trying to lure her away to their Top Secret projects. Job offers flew in from defense contractors around the Beltway. But she'd found her home.

She enjoyed life at the Pentagon, the headquarters and central hub of activity for the DoD. She was tasked to assist the branches of the armed services on network security issues, so she'd come down to Little Creek for the week, first to brief the higher-ups and then to get down in the dirt and play with the big boys. Figuratively speaking, of course. Although she'd work side-by-side with their IT specialists and network security administrators in rooting out the source of the attempted hacks, no way in hell was she falling into bed with any of them. No matter how attractive a man in uniform may be.

Lexi climbed into her SUV, dropping her briefcase and blazer onto the passenger seat. She adjusted her skirt as she started the engine, feeling the ache in her calves from walking around base in those damn heels all afternoon. Nothing sounded better right now than changing into some comfortable clothes and grabbing a drink at a bar down by the water.

She grabbed her buzzing cell phone from her briefcase, her best friend Kenley's picture flashing across the screen.

"Hi hun. Did you get my message?" she asked as she cranked up the AC. She pictured Kenley, petite with cascading brown curls, anxiously pacing back and forth in front of their favorite bar back in DC. The same place they were supposed to meet for drinks tonight before the game.

"Yeah, I just got it—I was stuck in meetings all day. You're down there all week?" Kenley moaned. "Who's going to come to the Nat's game with me

4

tonight?"

Lexi laughed. "I'm sure you'll find some poor guy to drag along."

"Two hours before the first pitch?"

"Call Cassidy," she said, referring to the third woman in their trio of friends. Tall and blonde, she was the exact opposite in looks from Lexi and Kenley, but the three of them had met just after college and were inseparable.

"No, she's tied up with what's-his-name."

"Literally?" Lexi asked with a chuckle. It was only five o'clock on a Monday night, but then again, you never knew with Cassidy.

"God, I hope not. TMI."

A smile played on Lexi's lips. If walls could talk, the ones in Cassidy's apartment would have enough stories to last a lifetime. "Sorry about the change in plans for tonight. I wasn't expecting to be sent down here—"

"But you're the best," Kenley finished with a sigh. "Can't I convince you to move over to the private sector? I could find you a kick-ass job. You'd pick your hours, decide which business trips you want—"

"Not a chance," Lexi laughed.

This must've been the twentieth time Kenley had pitched Lexi into abandoning the DoD for work at a large defense contractor. Although it might be fun working with her best friend, her career and interests were with the government. Fat chance she'd abandon that now after the years she'd put in, no matter how big the paycheck. With a few side IT projects that she was able to moonlight on—legally—she didn't really need the extra cash anyway.

"It was worth a shot," Kenley mumbled. "Oh

great, and now there's a creepy old guy checking me out. I should not be standing here alone in front of a bar."

"How old?"

"I don't know. Fifty. Too old. Ugh. All right, I'll head in and grab a drink myself. I feel like I'm on display out here."

"Tell him you have an extra ticket to the game," Lexi teased. "Maybe he could be your sugar daddy."

"Not a chance in hell. I'm so calling you back though if that creeper starts hitting on me."

"That's what best friends are for."

The two women hung up, and Lexi pulled out of the parking lot on base. She nodded at the guards as she exited. Damn, even they were good-looking. By Friday, she hoped to have this project wrapped up and be headed back to Northern Virginia. She was an expert at tracking down hackers and installing top-notch security systems impenetrable by anyone. If the hackers were in the US—doubtful—they'd be arrested. If they were on foreign soil, she'd see to it that they never made it past the firewalls and security systems she'd install at Little Creek. And maybe she'd give them a taste of their own medicine. A few lines of seemingly innocuous code, and their systems would be fried.

The day spent on base might've been perfect if it weren't for those damn SEALs all over the place. The men stationed at Little Creek reminded her a little too much of her former flame. She'd moved clear across the damn country to avoid seeing him again, abandoning her work at Coronado for life at the Pentagon. Not that her asshole of an ex had ever tried to track her down—he was scared senseless of commitment, of raising a family, of doing the right thing. And didn't that say a lot about the man—no, make that *boy*—that he was. He'd been young at the time, too, but any decent guy would've manned up. Taken responsibilities for his actions.

A pregnancy scare when she was twenty, after they'd been dating for a couple years, had shown his true colors. He wasn't the settling down type. Not the marrying kind. Certainly not fit to be a father. Maybe the false alarm had been for the best—she'd seen firsthand he wasn't the type of man to ever be happy about starting a family together, so she'd left. It might've broken her heart if she didn't hate him so damn much.

She'd hauled her ass across the country to avoid ever seeing him again. How's that for a reasonable reaction? God, if her parents had ever known the real reason she'd left California, they'd have a field day. He was never good enough, smart enough for her. She hadn't given a crap, but look where she'd ended up today. Single and alone at age twenty-nine.

Life at the Pentagon was good, but she missed the sea and warm weather. Washington just wasn't the same as laid-back California, and there were days when her homesickness hit her like a tidal wave, knocking her breathless. Maybe she'd look into transferring to a naval base here in Virginia one day. With seven years spent working her way up in the Department of Defense, she wasn't ready to jump ship. She'd stay with the DoD and still get to enjoy life near the water. She'd miss her friends and the life she'd built, but maybe a small part of her soul would finally feel at peace. Maybe.

One thing was for certain—she'd never, ever set

foot in Coronado again.

Six feet of solid muscle, warm brown eyes, and the hottest sex she'd ever had in her life had left her smitten with her first love. He was hotter than sin, a SEAL barely out of BUD/S when they'd first crossed paths. He'd taken her virginity, captured her heart, and promised her the world. Life had been pretty damn perfect until she'd thought she was pregnant. No question it was his. She'd never so much as let another man undress her before, let alone make love to her night after night.

The cold way he'd frozen up and questioned her loyalty to him made her want to rip his heart right out. To pound her fists against his chest until he apologized. To hurt him the cruel way he'd hurt her.

He'd attempted to ask for her forgiveness the next day, but it was too late. That ship had sailed, and she sure as hell didn't plan to ever speak to him again. She'd moved a week later, never once looking back on the life that could've been. The future she should've had. She didn't even know what the hell had happened to him. It's not like the movements and career of a SEAL were broadcast on the national news. And he sure as hell hadn't tried to follow her, contact her, or do a damn thing to win her back.

It was better this way. She had her busy career, her friends, and her condo in Arlington. An occasional date, but never anything serious. She certainly didn't need a man to come into her life and break her heart again. The SEALs at Little Creek had sent too many thoughts swirling around her mind—memories she couldn't forget, some memories she didn't want to forget. And one memory that chased her all these years later—of chocolate brown eyes that saw into her very soul. Then betrayed her when she needed him the most.

Chapter 2

Navy SEAL Christopher "Blade" Walters stared across the parking lot, dumbstruck, his hand frozen on the door of his black pick-up truck. As his calloused fingertips stilled against the hot metal, he jumped back, cursing as the heat burned his skin. The gorgeous woman walking across the lot on his base in Little Creek, VA had to be a mirage. A figment of his imagination. His mind must be playing tricks on him—long black hair, a figure to make grown men weep, and a saunter to her step that was both unaffected and somehow also screamed *come fuck me* clouded his vision.

What in the hell?

It was like he'd seen a ghost. An unwelcome, unwanted, yet sexy-as-hell reminder of the chick that haunted his dreams. Of the woman—the future—he'd had and lost.

Gorgeous, full breasts pushed up against a skimpy top that she had no right wearing around a military base filled with testosterone-driven men. They bounced as she walked, bringing to mind images of his ex riding him, night after night, her glorious full globes bouncing up and down as he fucked her into oblivion. She'd been young, innocent, and it had made him harder than steel to pleasure her body. To bring her to orgasm in *his* bed. Repeatedly. She'd be flushed and sated, gasping his name, and he'd flip her over and start again. Fucking hell.

The skirt this woman had on clung to her ass like a second skin, and if the apparition in the parking lot really were the woman he wished for, dreamt about, still tasted, he'd hike it up over her curvy hips, press her against his truck, and sink his way into heaven.

Two FA-18 Hornets screamed across the sky, momentarily drawing his attention upward. A lifetime ago, back in Coronado, he'd taken his girl to watch the military jets flying overheard nearly every weekend. They'd been young, in love, and he'd sneak her to a secluded spot on the beach for their own private viewing session. They'd picnic in the sand and then he'd make love to her at dusk in the back of his pick-up while the jets danced across the sky above. Hell if he hadn't thought of that shit in years. A brief pang of regret filled his chest, but he shook it off and glanced back at the ghost of the woman.

She climbed into an SUV a few rows over, not even noticing him, and he swore he could smell the scent of lavender wafting across the lot toward him. As if the scent of his ex had traveled thousands of miles across the US, strong and potent as a punch in the face, and found him here, in the parking lot on base of all damn places. As if this woman would have the same intoxicating scent as *her*.

She tucked her killer legs into the SUV, making his chest constrict at her familiar, intriguing femininity, and slammed the door shut, shielding her from his sight. The loss was painful, immediate. Unexplainable. He felt like a dick standing here, ogling that woman, but holy hell. She was a sight to behold. He blinked, visions of his past dancing across his eyelids. She was like a trip right down goddamn memory lane. Not one he cared to revisit, either. That door was closed—best never to be opened or even thought of again.

He climbed into his truck, his heart hammering in his chest, and white-knuckled the steering wheel, trying to get a damn hold of himself. Thank fuck the other guys weren't here to see him acting like this. Spooked over some woman of all things.

Like he needed this shit on top of everything else. His CO had pulled him aside after his SEAL team's drills that afternoon, asking for his assistance on some computer fuck-up on base. Apparently the secure systems had been repeatedly targeted by systematic attacks, source unknown. The IT staff always handled that sort of thing, but some fancy pants security specialist had been sent down from the Pentagon to brief the higher-ups and assess the vulnerabilities of their systems. Christopher had extensive background in computer forensics, so his CO asked him to sit in on the meetings tomorrow.

He grumbled as he turned the key in the ignition. He didn't have time to deal with other people's messes. Their SEAL team was finally all back together after the youngest man in their unit recovered from a serious injury sustained on their last mission. One month at Walter Reed up in Bethesda, and Evan "Flip" Jenkins was back down in Little Creek with the rest of them. Right where he belonged.

Those guys were like his brothers. Christopher and his SEAL team trained hard and fought harder. They worked in perfect synchronicity as one unit, both on and off the battlefield. Hours of PT and drills left them able to know one another's movements, read each other's thoughts. That tight bond was critical in battle and when running ops. He knew the other five guys inside and out and would give up his life for any of them.

Now that they were finally all back together, he didn't need the added distraction of worrying about network security on base—something the Navy's large IT and network security staff should be equipped to handle. And he sure as hell didn't need to be sitting here distracted over some damn mystery woman. The raven-haired beauty in the SUV had already driven off, and he was still sitting in his truck pining over the past like some chick. Hell.

Of the six men on his SEAL team, two were now officially taken. Evan and Patrick "Ice" Foster each had a gorgeous woman of their own. If Christopher hadn't seen those two tough, alpha males fall for their women with his own eyes, he wouldn't have believed it. For dudes destined to be single, they sure the hell seemed happier than shit now. Guess the saying was true, he thought with a smirk: the bigger they are, the harder they fall.

The rest of the men on his SEAL team were as single as him. And preferred it that way. Staying out of a relationship helped him stay out of trouble—

both on missions with his teammates and here at home. The fact that the memories of his haunted past were damn near tearing his heart out right now just proved how much a man like him was meant to be alone. The woman that filled all his dreams wasn't here. The woman whose violet eyes he saw whenever he had meaningless sex with some anonymous woman wasn't strolling around the parking lot on base.

That girl was back on the beaches of Coronado, long gone. She wasn't even a girl anymore because that shit was a damn lifetime ago. Hell, she probably had a husband and three kids by now. A family. That's what she wanted, right? Not some fuck-up who'd busted his ass in the Navy, somehow gotten into the SEALs, and deployed around the world half the damn time. Not a guy without a family, who barely had an idea what the word even meant.

Not the man who'd questioned her when she'd needed him most. Who'd taken the one person in his life he'd actually cared for and thrown her away. He'd been too much of a damned coward to even chase after her. To track her down and drag her back to Coronado where she belonged—with him. In his arms and in his bed. For forever and all that shit.

Hell, if that mix-up had gone down today, when he was older and wiser and had seen the world, he'd have moved heaven and earth to find her. To make things right between them. But back then he was young, stubborn. Foolish. And who was he kidding? Even if she was the best fucking part of his life, she was better off without him.

His father had walked out on him—it was damn near better that way since the only way he communicated was with his fists. His single mother did what she could to raise him right—not that she'd been around much either, working two jobs just to make ends meet. Joining the Navy right out of high school was the greatest thing he'd ever done. The Navy was the only thing that had brought him something solid, regimented, and real in his life. Something to fight for and believe in. As a SEAL, he protected the defenseless, came to the aid of those who couldn't help themselves. Accomplished missions when there was no one else to do the job. When failure was not an option. Maybe no one had been around to defend him from his old man when he was a kid, but he sure the hell would stand up for what was right and protect others now. His SEAL brothers were more like blood brothers—truer than any real family he'd ever known.

At thirty-three, Christopher had been in the military for fifteen years. Nearly half of his life had been devoted to service. He'd seen shit that other people would never even dream about. Fought with criminals, drug lords, and terrorists. Gone on missions he could never even talk about because they were so highly classified. Now he was spooked over some babe he'd spotted in the parking lot? Unbelievable.

This woman just happened to be his ex's sexier-than-sin lookalike. That shit didn't mean anything. No way in hell was he still pining over some lost love. This woman was just something to taunt him, reminding him of what he could never have. What he'd never deserved to begin with.

No way would Lexi Mattingly somehow end up here, clear on the other side of the country, waltzing around Little Creek like she owned the place. No way would he be lucky enough to have a chance with that woman more than once in his lifetime.

***

Lexi cruised along Atlantic Avenue in Virginia Beach, windows down, sea air blowing through her SUV. She tapped her fingers on the steering wheel to the beat of the music on her stereo. *Cruising* down the road was a pretty apt description of her drive to the hotel, and it sure beat sitting in traffic on the Beltway in DC. She inhaled the salty scent of the breeze and smiled. Fifteen minutes after leaving base, and she could already feel her head clearing and her body relaxing. Amazing what a little distance could do.

She pulled to a stop at the entrance of her oceanfront hotel, lining up behind the other cars full of people checking in. She felt bad for having to bail on her best friend tonight, but it wasn't like she'd exactly had a choice in the matter. Or like she could just pop back up to DC for the game. Kenley would probably meet a guy at Nat's Park, have a new boyfriend by the weekend, and be married and popping out cute babies by next year. The exact opposite of the way Lexi's own life would turn out, given the trajectory she'd been on so far.

A serious boyfriend who didn't want to settle down, followed by a string of meaningless relationships and orgasm-less sex? Check, check, and check. Wasn't her personal life fan-freaking-tastic at the moment?

She inched forward, admiring the gorgeous, sand-colored high-rise that loomed in front of her. Palm trees dotted the landscaping in front of the building while the Atlantic served as the spectacular backdrop. Every room had an oceanfront balcony, complete with a white railing. She may not have the house, yard, and white picket fence, but an oceanfront suite would do. She'd have to pay more than the government per diem allotted for her trip, but the view of the sparkling Atlantic was worth a few more dollars. As an in-demand security specialist who'd risen through the ranks at the Pentagon and who'd still been able to obtain several lucrative contract jobs from time-to-time, she had the cash to splurge.

Funny, she never pictured herself at twenty-nine as raking in the big bucks, advising the government and large corporations on network security. She'd hack into their systems, show them where their vulnerabilities lie, and collect a fat paycheck for her efforts. Lexi had always figured she'd end up as a wife and mom by the time she turned thirty, staying home for a few years while the kids were young before returning to the fast-paced workforce and lifestyle she was used to. She'd have a husband, a house, and a yard—not a sterile condo in the city that she had little time to decorate and even less time to spend in. She'd join the PTA and bake cupcakes for the school bake sales. Play with her kids. Be the picture of domestic bliss. And in her dreams, her children always had brown eyes like Christopher—not that she'd ever risk having kids with that bastard now.

It still smarted a little that all these years later she couldn't entirely get that man out of her mind. That no other man had even come close to meeting the impossible standards he'd set. With his ruggedly masculine features, intense personality, and larger-than-life career as a Navy SEAL, he'd come into her world and swept her away. Literally and figuratively. He'd been protective and caring. Supportive. A dominant alpha male who'd decided Lexi would be his—and she was. His efforts in the bedroom had left her breathless. He was the first man she'd ever been with and the absolute only man ever to make her come for him—to have her literally screaming his name in pleasure.

She blushed just thinking about her nights with him. Even though she still hated him with all of her heart, a tiny part of her yearned for his touch. His kiss. His ability to pleasure and drive her wild. The string of sexual encounters she'd had since then had been pointless. Pitiful even. Most guys didn't seem to notice if she was faking it when they took her to bed, but with Christopher? She'd been like putty in his hands. He cared for her but was possessive and dominating in the bedroom—driving her higher and higher as he sought her pleasure. He'd been her first—and he'd ruined her for other men.

She'd practically been a kid when she met him—just a foolish college girl with no idea what guys like him were like. He'd already been a SEAL when they met, the type of man used to attracting women wherever he went. She'd practically swooned when he'd noticed *her*. The sparks had been immediate, unstoppable. They'd clicked instantly, inexplicably. He was a tough, assertive SEAL; she was just an inexperienced college student.

But when they were together?

Fireworks. Explosions. Earth-shattering moments.

It was like the world stopped for everything but them.

The destructive crash landing of their relationship cut deep. Christopher turning his back on her when she'd been scared and helpless was not something she'd ever forgive or forget.

Good riddance.

She climbed out of the SUV, one of the valets rushing over to offer his assistance. She directed him to the suitcase in her trunk and grabbed her briefcase from the front seat. Her laptop and tablet were safely tucked inside, her briefings and notes from earlier stored on the hard drive. All of the classified information remained on the DoD computers, but the information she carried with her was still sensitive. Important. She'd lock her electronics in the safe in her room before she went out later tonight.

The valet directed her to a bellhop waiting to assist her. She followed him to the front doors of the massive hotel, noticing a man in dark sunglasses and a designer suit smoking a cigar at the far edge of the hotel's driveway. He seemed out of place amongst the casual tourists, but then again, she was in a business suit as well.

He watched her from afar, seeming to silently appraise her. His slicked back hair didn't have a strand out of place, and she could practically smell his strong cologne from thirty feet away. He was likely just some creep checking her out—what else was new? She was around men all day long in her field, and some respected women more than others. She wasn't going to stand around worrying about some slimy dude in a slick suit. She felt his eyes burning into her as she strode inside. It took everything in her not to turn around and flip him off. Just to let him know that she knew exactly what he was thinking.

Five minutes later, she was following the bellhop into the elevator, keycard in hand. In ten minutes, she planned to have her toes in the sand, drink in hand. There was no sense in letting regrets from the past ruin her evening. Maybe a few of the memories were nostalgic, but most of them were more bitter than sweet. She'd get the job done, and get on with her life. Just like she always had. All she had to do was make it through the week around all those damn SEALs.

Chapter 3

Christopher parked his truck in a garage near the beach an hour later and sauntered down the sidewalk to Anchors, a popular Virginia Beach bar that his SEAL team frequented. The bustling hangout was always filled with single military guys and local women alike, making it the perfect place to carouse. He and his buddies usually grabbed drinks there every week, chasing after the pretty ladies and more often than not taking one home for the night. Their team of six single men was now down to four, but hell. He could spend a few hours unwinding with them after the day he'd had.

He'd changed after work into well-worn jeans and a tee shirt, but that didn't lessen the stares of the women as he stepped inside. They loved a man in a uniform, but with his short, military-style cropped hair and build of a SEAL, he didn't exactly blend in even while wearing civilian clothes. His muscular

21

frame filled out anything he wore. Normally he loved the attention, but tonight he just needed a drink to clear his damn head.

Christopher and his buddies had met their fair share of women at Anchors over the years, but lately, he'd only spend a night or two with a woman before moving on to the next. No sense in leading anyone on when he knew he wasn't going to be around for the long haul. He'd be upfront with his intentions, saving both him and the woman he took home a helluva lot of grief. He was ashamed to admit it, but many of those women didn't care one way or another. They wanted the allure of spending the night in the bed of a SEAL, and who was he to turn down an attractive lady's offer? He sure wasn't looking for a relationship. His one bitter breakup years ago had left him enough heartache for a lifetime. Not that he'd fucking admit that to anyone. Ever.

He was running late in meeting the guys, his mind a jumbled mess ever since leaving base earlier. The woman from the parking lot haunted him. What the hell was that about anyway? He'd gone damn near ten years without seeing or hearing from Lexi. He thought about her, sure. What red-blooded male wouldn't? Her jet black hair, violet eyes, and smoking hot body were the stuff wet dreams were made of. And she'd been his. Not some fantasy woman. A real flesh-and-blood woman who'd let him make her his own, take her to bed every night, and teach her just how pleasurable sex could be.

Christ. She was a fucking virgin when he'd met her. No wonder no other woman ever seemed as sweet, innocent, and genuine. He'd been her first— her first serious boyfriend, first lover, first everything.

Not to mention the first asshole that had broken her heart.

But he'd moved on. Learned to live with his regret. The past was in the past. Now some babe he'd spotted for only an instant had his heart skittering to a stop and his mind replaying movie reels of what had happened a lifetime ago. What he needed was a couple of beers and some harmless flirting to keep the memories from churning through his mind. To keep the ghosts from his past at bay. That shit would haunt anyone.

In the far corner of Anchors, he finally spotted some of the guys on his team: Brent "Cobra" Rollins was nursing a beer, his eyes flicking with interest around the crowded bar. Mike "Patch" Hunter was chatting with two young co-eds, and Evan was sitting with his girlfriend, Alison, his arm slung casually over the strawberry blonde's shoulder. Alison was a sweet little thing, a nurse at the local hospital. Although Christopher sure as shit wasn't the settling down type, he could see why Evan would be interested in her. That guy had a stable family background and wanted a wife and kids. He was the youngest guy on the team, and although he'd seen a lot in his years as a SEAL, he wasn't jaded about life the way the rest of them were.

After a serious injury in the field just over a month ago, Evan looked happier and healthier than ever. With the pretty nurse on his arm, it made complete and total sense. Those two had a bit of a slow start, with Evan constantly chasing after her. Or was it Alison chasing him, secretly wanting to be caught? Christopher smirked. The explosion that had blown up the vehicle Evan was driving while on their last mission had been brutal, but if Evan's injuries were what had been needed to finally bring him and Alison together, Christopher supposed that it had worked out for the best. Those two seemed meant for one another.

But as for Christopher needing a wife or a family? Not a fucking chance.

The door opened behind him, and he realized he'd been standing there lost in thought. First the parking lot, now this? He was going to have to turn in his man card after tonight.

Hell.

Matthew "Gator" Murphy walked into Anchors, slapping him on the back. "What's up, Blade?" he asked, calling Christopher by his nickname.

"Just got here, bro."

"And we got here just in time," Matthew crooned.

Christopher barely got a word out before Matthew drawled hello to a group of women, sauntering off and leaving him standing there alone. The dude sure knew how to lay on the southern charm. One of the women glanced Christopher's way and pouted, but he wasn't in the mood to flirt with some chick he'd likely never see again. Especially one acting like a sullen teenager.

Hell. When did he turn into such an old man?

Christopher scowled and headed over to where the other guys were. The only man missing from their team was Patrick. He had a young son and had just started a relationship with Rebecca a few months ago, so he was usually absent from their guys' nights at Anchors. Patrick and Rebecca each had a kid, so that didn't really allow them to spend their nights hanging out in bars. Not that Patrick needed to nowadays anyway since he had a woman of his own. That guy was completely smitten with her. The guys liked to rib him about it, since Patrick's nickname was Ice. Rebecca had broken through that ice-cold persona, and after an incident earlier in the summer where a stalker had been after her, the two of them were inseparable.

With the ways things were going lately, Christopher felt like he'd be the last man standing. Scratch that. No way was Brent going to end up in a relationship.

Christopher gestured to the waitress for a beer as he joined the other guys. Her eyes sparked with interest as her gaze trailed over his muscular physique, but he gave her a brief nod and moved toward his friends.

"What'd the CO need you for?" Brent asked, eyebrows raised, as Christopher sank down into an empty chair at their table.

"I've got to attend some damn meeting tomorrow morning about network security on base."

"And miss the drills out on the water?"

Christopher shrugged, taking a swig from his beer. "Guess so. We have plenty of IT staff, but they wanted me to weigh in on a few things. Some hotshot from the Pentagon is down here this week. Apparently someone's been trying to hack into the secure systems."

"And they needed your sorry ass?" Brent asked.

Mike chuffed out a laugh. "Sic Christopher and his computer voodoo on them, and they'll be chasing their tails around trying to figure out what hit them."

"Damn straight," Evan laughed.

Christopher smirked. He could hack into damn

near anything. That's how he earned his nickname, "Blade." Some woman he'd met fresh out of BUD/S didn't know what a hacker was and thought he literally hacked into shit with a knife or something. The men in his class never let him live it down, and the name "Blade" had stuck.

He'd helped Patrick track down the man stalking Rebecca earlier in the summer, hacking into credit card databases to glean info on the suspect. No one had been the wiser that he'd been there, but the team had secured a plan to track the sick bastard down. He didn't feel the slightest bit of remorse when what he did was for the greater good. No way would he let a man harm a woman or child, and their entire team had helped Patrick guard Rebecca and track down her stalker.

Mike turned his attention back to them, the two women he was chatting with wandering off, giggling. "I think I saw her."

"Her?" Christopher asked in confusion. His eyes drifted to the women who'd just left.

"The hotshot from DC. Hotter than hell was more like it. I usually prefer blondes, but J wouldn't turn her down if she came knocking."

Brent guffawed and nearly spit out his beer. "What the fuck did she look like?"

"You would've liked her," Mike said, his shit-eating grin spreading across his face.

"Killer tits?" Brent asked, a wicked gleam in his eye.

"Easy, guys," Evan chuckled. "Ali's not going to want to hang out with me here anymore."

"Aw, hell. She knows you only have eyes for her," Mike said. He looked sheepishly at Alison. "Sorry."

Alison laughed at his obvious discomfort. "I'm sure some of my nurse friends at the hospital would love to meet a Navy SEAL if you're looking for a date, Mike. Maybe I could invite them along next time?"

"I could let a nurse tend to my wounds," Brent agreed. "How's that working out for you, Evan?"

Alison turned about ten different shades of red. Christopher apologized to her for Brent's behavior as Brent winked and excused himself, chasing after a blonde in a tight red dress that had just walked by their table. For the love of God.

"He's terrible," Evan muttered.

"He was just teasing me," Alison said, still looking rather embarrassed. "I don't think I'd set up my friends with him though. How about you guys?" she asked, glancing between Christopher and Mike. "I could introduce you to someone."

"Hell yeah," Mike agreed. "Tell me about these slutty nurses."

"Who said they were slutty?" Alison asked, laughing as Evan pulled her closer. He lightly kissed the top of her head.

"In my mind, they totally are. You in?" he asked, glancing over at Christopher

"Nah," Christopher muttered. "I'm going to grab another drink."

He stood, leaving Mike quizzing Alison about the single women she worked with. That's all he needed—one more man tied down. The next thing he knew, Matthew, Brent, and him would be the only single guys left. The rest of them would be off playing house with their girlfriends, dicks in their hands. Like he fucking needed that.

Christopher ground his teeth together as a drunk guy bumped into him, nearly spilling his beer all over Christopher's tee shirt. Christopher neatly sidestepped him and continued on his path toward the bar. Man, he was getting too old for this. What had been fun years ago was seeming a helluva lot more like work these days—drunk guys chasing after scantily clad women. Young college girls hitting on him. Crowds of people looking only to hook up for the night.

Jesus. The next thing he knew, he'd be settling down into domestic bliss like Patrick and Evan with their women, happy to avoid this scene altogether.

Right.

He worked his way through the crowd at the bar, trying to decide if he wanted another long neck or something a little stronger. The burn of some liquor wouldn't be a bad thing tonight. Might even chase all those ghosts away. He finally decided that maybe a shot or two would calm his frayed nerves, when the scent of lavender hit him like a bolt of lightning. He stiffened, his entire body jolting to high alert. What in the hell?

It was sweet. Fragrant. Intoxicating.

Unforgettable.

"Well, I'll be damned," a sweet, feminine voice said. The steely undercurrent of the tone wasn't lost on him.

His heart nearly stuttered to a halt, tension coursing through his muscular frame as he clenched his jaw. He was frozen in place, save for his dick, which was suddenly rising to attention. That fucking voice that haunted his dreams. That scent. That woman.

He turned, already lost in a pair of violet eyes.

Lexi.

And she looked madder than hell.

Chapter 4

Lexi stilled as shock shot straight through her, electricity coursing from her head all the way down to her toes. She was frozen in place, her heart thumping erratically. Aside from the few words she'd uttered, she couldn't get her brain to properly function at the moment to add anything else. Not anything coherent at least. Simultaneous undercurrents of anger and rage within her competed with surprise, confusion, and hurt. She didn't think she'd still feel betrayed seeing him all these years later, but there it was. Her past had come back to haunt her—all six feet, two hundred plus pounds of him was right in front of her.

Bigger and better than ever.

He was tall, broad, even bigger than she remembered. Nearly ten years had bulked him up, giving him large biceps and pecs, a broad muscular chest that she had simultaneous urges to sink into and throttle in frustration. Pounds of muscle laid beneath that tee shirt he had on. Well-worn jeans clung to muscular thighs. At one point of her life she'd had every inch of his body memorized—now there were muscles on top of muscles, ridges and dips and all sorts of new, interesting things to explore. Hell, even his forearms were sexy—corded muscle with veins that stood out against his tanned skin, leading to his tough, very male hands. Hands that had once thoroughly explored her entire body.

She flushed as she gazed at his powerful stature—as memories bombarded her. His tightly leashed strength was contained, the power coursing through his muscular body somehow both attractive and arousing. His scent hit her like a ton of bricks—it was fresh and clean, like he'd just showered. Memories swirled through her mind of them showering together in his apartment, years ago—his large frame dripping wet beneath the shower head; her body trembling for him; his fingers, tongue, and finally his cock between her legs. It nearly took her breath away just recalling the power he held over her—the way he commanded and pleasured her body in a way no man ever had before. In a way no man ever could since.

His face showed a few lines that had appeared with age, and it was more chiseled than in her memories. That angular jaw, the soft lips, those freaking gorgeous brown eyes. He was so big and ruggedly handsome it almost hurt just to look at him. She wanted to step back from his intense stare, to shy away—to move anywhere that she couldn't feel the heat radiating off his body. But she wasn't that innocent girl anymore. She'd met Christopher when she was nineteen—young, inexperienced, naive. Nearly ten years had gone by. She wasn't the same woman now.

Her momentary feelings of shock at meeting his penetrating brown gaze, however, were quickly replaced with anger. The bitterness she'd felt after he'd questioned her years ago, the cold way he'd stomped out the door when she'd worriedly told him she may be pregnant, the fear and loneliness she'd felt as she sat alone sobbing in her apartment—that wasn't something you ever forgot. Those weren't things you ever could forgive.

So what if the suspected pregnancy had turned out to be just a false alarm? She wanted Christopher there at the store with her buying boxes of pregnancy tests—she wanted his hand to be the one she held as she waited for one or two little pink lines to appear. It didn't matter that he'd returned hours later, early the next morning, pounding on her door. It was over.

Maybe Christopher could handle all the macho, alpha male stuff, running around with his SEAL buddies on dangerous missions, but when she'd needed him just to be a man? Just to be her boyfriend and not some military hero? He'd freaked out and bailed. Literally left her standing alone in her apartment while he got his shit together. God only knows where he went, but by the time he returned? She was done.

She'd slammed the door in his face and never spoken to him again.

"Lexi," he said, finally stunned out of whatever trance he'd been in as he'd locked eyes with her. His voice was warm, rich, and smooth. Hearing it felt like sipping hot chocolate on a cold day or coming home again—it warmed her all over, from her inside out, sending heat and awareness bursting forth from her center and coursing over her skin. She flushed as it filled her heart and chest with a longing she hadn't felt in a decade. With a need she couldn't describe.

"Christopher." She hoped he didn't hear the shakiness in her voice. Goosebumps spread over her skin. No other man had ever had this effect on her. No other man overwhelmed her simply with his presence, just with her name on his lips. The way he uttered it was almost a cross between a plea and a prayer. He didn't move a muscle, but it felt like his entire body was reeling her in.

"What are you doing here?" His low voice burned with an intensity she didn't want to examine too closely. Confusion clouded his face. Deep brown eyes held her hostage. The sounds from the rest of Anchors seemed to fade into the background, the clinking of glasses and animated conversations just a dull roar. She had to be dreaming. Nine years had gone by, but when she saw him, it was like she was transported through time.

Except in that fairy tale, he'd betrayed her and left. He was no Prince Charming, and this was no happily-ever-after.

"I was just wondering the same thing." She crossed her arms and narrowed her gaze. Had he tracked her down here? Impossible. Why wait nearly a decade and then follow her down to Virginia Beach?

"What you're doing here?" he asked, a hint of amusement spreading across his too-handsome-for-his-own-good face. Despite his shock in seeing her, the edge of his lips quirked with a hint of a smile.

Cocky, arrogant bastard.

"No," she snapped, irritated. "What the hell you're doing here."

"Hallucinating, apparently."

"Excuse me?"

"Lexi, my God. I haven't seen you in ten years." She couldn't read the expression on his face, couldn't see a hint of any emotion in his dark eyes. For a man she once knew intimately, completely, they were now perfect strangers. He had an entire life she knew nothing about. For a man who'd once been her best friend and lover, it was almost painful to be so awkwardly unacquainted. Her drycleaner knew more about her life than Christopher did. They meant that little to each other now.

"And whose fault is that?"

He had the decency to look embarrassed, and her chest tightened. It was most certainly in anger. No way in hell did she feel regret at no longer knowing this man. "You're stationed at Little Creek." It wasn't a question. There was no other reason he'd be clear across the country at a bar frequented by the local military men. The chances of him being randomly sent here the exact same week as her were slim-to-none. She didn't believe in coincidences.

"Yes." His jaw ticked.

"Since when?"

He cleared his throat. "Eight years."

Goosebumps spread across her flesh. Blood pounded in her ears. He'd left a year after her. Why would he ever leave Coronado? The only reason she could come up with was because she'd left, too. But the real reason was a damn mystery, because he'd been the one to walk out. She was about to lose her shit. Even when she returned home, Virginia Beach was only a four-hour drive from DC. She came here damn near every summer with her girlfriends. Hell.

Kenley's parents owned a condo near the beach. Lexi and Kenley had just stayed there over Memorial Day weekend a few months ago. She thought she'd put the whole damn country between them, and if she wanted, she could be down in an afternoon, just like that. It was actually painful to think he'd been so close all this time. To think that they could've....

Could've what?

Had he known that she'd come to DC? No, if he'd come after her, he'd have done exactly that. Come. After. Her. Come to DC, tracked her down at the Pentagon, looked her up in the DoD personnel files. None of that would be difficult for a SEAL with connections. Or for a man intent on finding the woman he once loved. Christopher was here on the East Coast, in Little Creek, for the Navy and the Navy alone. None of it had a damn thing to do with her moving here.

Lexi glared at him. "You ran out on me," she accused. "On us."

"I was just a dumb kid back then—"

"I was a kid back then. Just a college student! You were some hotshot SEAL who'd already seen the world. You had a career, a life, everything! But you couldn't handle a relationship."

"For the love of God—"

The bartender interrupted, asking for their order, and Christopher shot him a deadly glare. The bartender's gaze flicked over to her, uncertain. Christopher calmly reached for her elbow to lead her away from the crowded area.

"Don't touch me!"

He flinched, looking as if she'd slapped him. Maybe she should. It would feel pretty damn good after all these years. He sure as hell would never hit a woman, but slapping him across that handsome face was sounding better and better with every passing second. In fact, with all the anger and rage coursing through her at the moment, she wanted to pound her fists on his chest, to make him actually feel something for a change. That cold-hearted bastard had walked out on her when she'd needed him. When she'd been terrified, he'd simply turned around and walked out the door, their years together over, just like that.

The only problem was, with all those pounds of muscle on his six-foot frame, her pummeling him would probably be as effective as a kitten batting at a ball of yarn. It might make her feel better, but it sure wouldn't hurt him—physically or otherwise. She crossed her arms, growing more defensive with each passing second. What the hell was he doing here, anyway? He was supposed to be back in California, right where she'd left him.

He glanced over to a table in the far corner of the bar, and she saw a group of people watching them with interest—two other guys who had to be SEALs, judging from their massive builds, and an attractive, strawberry blonde women. The men had huge grins on their faces, and only the woman looked slightly concerned. Well wasn't that fan-freaking-tastic. Now they had an audience to watch their ten-year reunion.

Brushing past Christopher, who was still entirely too close for comfort, she slid onto an empty barstool and ordered a shot of whiskey to calm her shaky nerves. Normally she was a beer girl, but tonight? Not a chance.

She hadn't seen a ring on his finger, but SEALs didn't always wear them. If he'd freaked out on her then married the next woman he took to bed, she'd freaking kill him. Right here in this goddamn bar in front of half the Navy. Anger coursed through her at even the mere idea of Christopher with another woman. Ten damn years had gone by—of course he'd had other women. Probably hundreds of them. She was just one in a lifetime of the endless stream of females he'd chase after.

Christopher growled behind her, edging closer as the bartender appraised her with interest. She'd changed after work into a strappy little sundress. It wasn't revealing, per se, but the way it hugged her curves never had men complaining. So now Christopher was jealous because some young college kid was eyeing her appreciatively? Too freaking bad. He'd lost his right to have an opinion on anything she did when he'd walked away years ago. The hell with him.

"Make it two," he said in a low voice, throwing some cash down on the bar.

The bartender nodded and turned to pour their shots. He was cute, in a young, scruffy-looking kind of way.

Christopher wedged himself next to where she sat perched on the barstool, his hulking frame sending her body pulsing with awareness. He was too big. Too male. Too cocky for his own damn good. She ought to refuse his unspoken offer to buy her a drink, but what did she care? One shot, and she was outta here. She just needed a little liquid courage to will herself to walk away.

"He's not your type," Christopher murmured, ducking low so that his lips brushed against her ear. His scent surrounded her, and his mouth at her ear sent a thousand different memories stirring deep inside. Whispered promises. Gentle commands. Words shared between lovers.

She actually shivered at his closeness.

One large hand came to rest on her back, the heat from it searing her flesh. Her nipples tightened as her chest rose and fell, and Christopher's gaze slid to her breasts. Damn her body for betraying her. His eyes raked back up her body, his look incendiary. Liquid heat coursed through her, sending heat coiling down from her center until arousal dampened her panties. She wanted to squirm away, to turn and leave, but she wouldn't give him the satisfaction. Wouldn't let him know how much he affected her still.

"And how would you know?" she asked.

"I know exactly what your type is." His voice was dark. Full of lust and desire. His large hand splayed across her upper back was possessive. Enticing. He was about to send her up in flames.

"Like hell you do."

His lips brushed against her ear. "You don't need a boy like him; you need a man."

"Maybe I already have one," she huffed, trying to rile him up. No freaking way was she letting him bait her, gain the upper hand. Christopher couldn't affect her at all anymore—the walls she'd put up over the past decade were impenetrable, even by him.

A beat passed, and his breath tickled her skin. He edged even closer, his chest against her bare shoulder, his lips brushing against the shell of her ear.

She shuddered.

"I don't see a ring on your finger."

"And big surprise, I don't see one on yours," she retorted.

"There's no other woman, Lexi. Hell, I can still taste you all these years later. Hear you cry out my name. If we weren't in a goddamn bar surrounded by all these people, I'd take you right here. Prove you wrong."

"Don't kid yourself. I haven't thought of you once since I left California."

She flashed a glance his way, and his eyes flared in anger as he straightened, carefully schooling his expression. The heat from where his hand had been still burned into her skin. Marking her. Making her long for more of his scalding touch.

Everywhere.

"Where do you work?" he demanded.

"The Pentagon."

"We're a long way from Washington."

"So we are."

"You're visiting base?" he asked.

Years ago, a computer whiz even back in college, she'd gotten an internship at Coronado. Having Christopher working there too was exciting. She was just a college intern, and he was a larger-than-life, sexier-than-hell Navy SEAL. But now? The thought of even walking around the same building with him in it made her feel dizzy and ill. Like his mere presence there would be too much for her to handle. They didn't need a wall between them, they needed an entire country. Preferably a few continents.

"Just for the week."

A flash of respect shown in his eyes. She turned away before he asked her more questions.

No way was she sticking around Anchors, even if she did convince Christopher to leave her alone. Not with his very presence causing her body to short-circuit. Not with the brown eyes she'd dreamt about boring into hers. She couldn't breathe around him—couldn't think, couldn't stop the instinctive response she'd always had when he was near.

The bartender set their shot glasses in front of them, nodding at Christopher when he waved off needing change.

The whiskey burned down her throat.

She felt hot, too hot. Uncomfortable in her own skin. Long forgotten memories she didn't want to face were churning to the surface—good memories, bad memories. All the other ones in between.

"I've got to go," she said, sliding down off the barstool.

"Like hell you do," Christopher said, lightly catching her waist in one large hand. He was massive. Overwhelming. Irresistible. "You disappear ten years ago and then suddenly want to act like nothing happened between us?"

"You disappeared on me, remember?" she asked, her voice steely. "You walked out of my apartment like I meant nothing to you."

"Lexi—"

"Goodbye, Christopher."

She pulled away from his searing grip on her waist and stormed off, nearly bumping into another wall of solid muscle. She jumped back, the hairs on the back of her neck tingling as Christopher came up behind her. The heat from his large frame radiated off him, and her breath caught. Just. Freaking. Perfect. Now she was stuck between two burly SEALs.

"This isn't over, Lexi," Christopher growled.

"Like hell it isn't," she snapped, glaring over her shoulder at him. Thick arms crossed against his solid chest. Soft cotton hugged his pecs. Light stubble covered his clenched jaw. He looked about as immobile as a mountain. And as freaking gorgeous as a Greek God.

"Aw, hell, darlin'. Christopher's not that bad."

She turned back and rolled her eyes at the man in front of her, obviously buddies with her ex. He was not one of the men from the table earlier that had been watching them. Did Christopher know everyone in this damn place?

"He's worse," she muttered, brushing past him as he stepped out of her way, chuckling.

She felt Christopher's eyes burning into her back as she stalked off, and she threw an extra little saunter into her step. Screw him. No way was he going to chase after her with his friend watching. He had way too much pride.

Her heart pounded in her chest as she pushed open the door to Anchors and stepped out into the cool night. The evening air bathed her overheated flesh, and she took a deep breath, sucking in precious oxygen. She felt shaken to her core running into him. The moment he'd met her eyes, she knew she had to leave. Her body didn't care that he was a bastard—it screamed for his power and strength to be moving over her—inside her. For him to kiss her like he once had and steal her breath away.

It took absolutely every ounce of her willpower to walk rather than sprint out of there, head held high, but so help her, she was not spending another second in that man's presence. The possibility of running into Christopher again while she was in town was unnerving. Unsettling. It sent her mind reeling and her stomach tumbling to the ground.

No, no, no.

This was all wrong. Tomorrow everything would be fine. She'd stick to her meetings with the IT staff, avoiding the SEALs roaming around base, handle the attempted hacks to the network, and make a clean exit at the end of the day. One week here, and she'd be done.

No problem.

If only she could convince her heart of that, too.

Chapter 5

"You piss off another lady?" Matthew drawled as Christopher slammed his shot glass down on the bar. Lexi's very empty barstool still sat beside him, and he bit out a curse.

"Just a ghost from my past," he muttered.

Sonofabitch.

Matthew laughed and ordered two beers, drawing the attention of a few women seated nearby. Christopher couldn't care less. There was only one woman he gave a damn about, and she'd just strutted right back into and out of his life. Fucking hell.

"You sure have a way with the women," Matthew needlessly pointed out.

"Right. Usually I don't know them well enough to piss them off that much."

"What about that crazy chick from California?"

Christopher's gaze slid back to Matthew. He didn't say a word, just waited for it to click.

"Shit. That was her?"

"In the flesh."

"What the hell's she doing here?"

"I'll be damned if I know."

He could run after her, chase her down. She couldn't have gotten that far. With her sleek black hair trailing over the strappy little dress she had on, she'd stand out against all the too blonde, too tanned women running around Virginia Beach. Hell. She was as fucking gorgeous as he remembered—more so, even. Pouty lips, full breasts, curvy hips, and those violet eyes he'd gotten lost in. His hands itched to trace over her soft skin, getting reacquainted with the curves he'd once known so well. He longed to taste her—both her sweet lips and what lie beneath those lacy panties she always wore. Did she still have a thing for that sexier-than-sin lace? Or had she switched to skimpy thongs or satiny panties instead? The thought of not knowing was driving him mad. Adrenaline surged through him, making him want to roar in frustration. Urging him to act on locating her, taking her home, making her his again.

Fucking hell.

What would be the point of chasing after her? She obviously didn't want a thing to do with him. He was the one with wounds from a lifetime ago. Lexi had moved onward and upward.

Not that he'd spotted a ring on her finger or anything.

A tiny dash of hope sparked inside his chest, instantly gone as quick as it came. Who the hell was he kidding? He'd had a shot with this girl and blown it. So what if he'd carried a torch for her for years. So what if he'd never been in a serious relationship again because it was her that he wanted. Needed. So what if he bedded numerous women over the years, trying to forget the only one that his body craved.

He groaned.

Her lavender scent lingered in the air, taunting him. Lavender. The same scent he'd noticed in the parking lot on base. Jesus. That had been her he'd seen earlier. He'd gone nearly a decade without seeing the woman only to have her show up in his life twice in the same day? No way in hell—

"I see you met the big shot security specialist," Mike said, sauntering up to them, beer in hand. "What'd you do to piss her off? I've never seen a woman run away from you so fast."

Matthew laughed, handing Christopher one of the beers he'd just ordered. Christopher glared at them both, taking a long pull from the bottle. Big shot security specialist. What the—

"You know her?" Matthew asked, a smile threatening to break out across his face.

"I saw her earlier," Mike said. "Total babe."

"And where'd you see her?" Matthew asked casually, looking like the cat that had eaten the canary.

"On base."

Christopher's conversation with his CO that afternoon came crashing back into his mind. Lexi was the one he'd be meeting with tomorrow?

Sonofabitch.

His gut churned as his groin tightened. No way in hell was his next conversation with Lexi going to be in front of all of Little Creek. Not with the way her wide violet eyes had gazed into his—not with the way she'd shivered on the barstool as his lips brushed against her ear.

Lexi, unaffected by him?

Not a chance in hell.

His SEAL training gave him an ability to read people, to watch all the tiny signs people unknowingly gave off. They all had to be attuned to their surroundings when running ops, following their instincts, and basing decisions on the people around them. On a mission it could mean the difference between life and death. Not that it had taken years in the military to read when a woman wanted him. Unbeknownst to Lexi, she'd been giving off signs the second he crowded her space at the bar. Her pupils had dilated, her breathing had hitched. Her nipples had tightened as his eyes slid over her gorgeous body in that sexy little sundress she had on. Holy hell, if he'd ever wanted to undress a woman with his eyes before, it had been tonight. He'd give anything to peel off that dress, to see the lacy lingerie and smoking hot body beneath.

He needed to kiss her rosy lips, to touch the miles of smooth skin running over that curvy body. To slide those straps down on her sundress and lave attention on her swollen breasts. They were round, full, and made just to tempt him. He needed to tease her the way he'd spent hours doing a lifetime ago, making her tremble and shudder for him. His chest clenched as he thought of her slamming the door in his face when he'd tried to return the following morning. He needed to hold her close and keep her safe. To breathe in her lavender scent and the sweet smell that was pure Lexi. To explain that on his life, he'd never meant to hurt her. That he'd gone damn near a decade unable to forgive himself for what he'd done.

"She was pretty fine," Matthew drawled, jerking his mind back to the present.

Christopher's eyes shifted to him, taking in the smirk on his face. "For the love of God," he muttered, clenching his fists together. "She's off limits."

"Easy," Matthew laughed. "Just making sure we're all on the same page."

"And what page is that?" Mike asked, his brow furrowed.

"The hotshot security specialist is Christopher's ex."

Mike let out a low whistle. "As in the chick from California he's always talking about?"

"For fuck's sake, I told you about her one time."

"And that's one time more than you've talked about any other woman," Matthew quipped, making Christopher want to punch that shit-eating grin right off his face.

"Hell, she's got our boy all worked up," Mike said.

"You two need to get laid," Christopher muttered, standing up.

Adrenaline surged through his veins, a mixture of need and regret filling his chest. Pinning Lexi against her SUV in the parking lot and kissing her senseless didn't seem like a reasonable way to solve their problems, but damn. Seeing her had sparked a craving in his body that had been lying dormant for years. He'd been with more than his fair share of the opposite sex, but never had he thoroughly possessed a woman as he had Lexi. Never had a woman made him come so undone, made him need to seek her pleasure over and over again until they were both satiated beyond belief.

His groin tightened just thinking about her curvy body—those full breasts, those hips a man wanted to grip as he drove into her, and that delicious ass that he wanted to sink his teeth into.

Hell. He was as hard as a goddamn rock.

He needed answers from Lexi, and he needed to make amends. He needed to take her to bed and keep her there forever. The guilt he'd carried with him for a decade wouldn't be put to rest until he talked to her, told her the truth. And if that didn't change anything? Well then, so be it. He'd either be able to work things out or finally move the hell on.

He left his half-empty bottle on the bar and grunted a goodbye, pushing his way through the crowd. Five minutes had gone by, but she couldn't have gotten too damn far. Maybe he hadn't gone after the girl years ago, but not even the laughter of his SEAL team trailing behind him would stop him tonight.

***

Lexi walked down the street to her SUV, wishing she'd brought a damn jacket. The heat from the late summer day had given way to a cool evening, with a breeze blowing in off the water. She dodged around a couple kissing on the sidewalk and tried not to groan. She'd been young and in love once, too—a freaking lifetime ago. Moonlit walks down by the water were a hell of a lot more fun when you weren't alone.

She sure the hell would never trust a man enough to ever give her heart to him again. Nope, Lexi was destined to be alone. Maybe it was better that way. If she was married to her career, she'd never have to worry about her heart being shattered again.

She rubbed her hands up and down her arms as goosebumps coated her skin. And they sure weren't the same type of goosebumps that had trailed down her arms as Christopher murmured in her ear earlier, either.

What the hell was that about anyway?

Of all the times she'd imagined running into him again, telling him off, hurting him the way he'd hurt her, she'd always had the upper hand in her mind's eye. She'd be the one spouting off insults a mile a minute, sharp words coming off her tongue, and he'd be the one left standing alone in shock as she'd sauntered off, leaving him in the dust. Giving him a taste of his own medicine.

In all her fantasies, she'd never stood before him shell-shocked, in disbelief, as her heart slowly began to unravel once more. She'd been strong and vehement. Adamant that he'd wronged her. She'd never felt disarmed and vulnerable. So completely raw.

She'd been mad at the man for a decade, and the first time she'd set eyes on him in nearly ten years, her entire body had gone on high alert. And not the fending off an attack, put up all defenses kind of alert. The warmth surging through her, arousal pooling in her core, and tingles covering every inch of her skin was more of a sweet surrender.

Holy hell.

When he'd crowded into her space at the bar, scalded her back with the burning touch of his hand, and bent over to whisper into her ear, she thought she'd combust. For a man she now considered to be jackass numero uno of the entire male species, did he have to be so goddamn enticing? It was frustratingly curious the way she responded to him. Her entire body felt like it might just go up in flames with one more of his smoldering glances.

He'd wanted her, too. That much was apparent. The heat in his eyes, his lingering touch…. How the hell he could live with himself after hurting her years ago was a damn mystery. He sure didn't seem to be in the mood to chat with the way his lips had brushed against her ear and his body had crowded hers. Did he seriously think she'd go home with him after all that had happened between them? Not a freaking chance in hell.

Kenley was still at the damn game, so she couldn't call her. Cassidy was always an option, but she'd tell Lexi to sleep with Christopher just to get it out of her system. Ironically, the only person she really wanted to talk to was the man himself. To demand an explanation. And for the second time, she'd walked out on him. It's not like—

"Lexi!"

She froze mid-step, her stomach flip-flopping. Only the deep timbre of one man could reverberate through her entire body, sending her insides reeling like that. There was no way in hell Christopher would come after her. What would his SEAL buddies think? She had to be imagining—

"Lexi!"

He was behind her in an instant, his fingers encircling her wrist as he spun her around. His touch burned into her skin, but she didn't pull away as her mouth dropped open in shock. Black cotton spanned his chest, hugging every inch of muscle in the moonlight. The scruff of his five o'clock shadow highlighted his chiseled jaw—but those eyes. His searing gaze burned into her very soul.

"What are you—?"

She never finished her question, because muscular arms encased her, pulling her into that inviting chest. His heat surrounded her, warding off the chill of the night air, shielding her from the breeze blowing in off the ocean. She tilted her head back, trying to search his face for some explanation of what exactly was happening, and his mouth instantly covered hers.

He tasted of whisky and man—all dark, delectable, and intoxicating. His clean scent surrounded her, and she whimpered as his lips moved softly against hers. Her hands found his chest, and she clutched desperately at his tee shirt. He rained soft kisses over her skin, completely at odds with his mass of muscle and sheer strength. She trembled in his arms, not knowing if she should come with him or run away from his particular brand of torture—entire nights full of searing kisses, teasing caresses, and screaming orgasms. Satisfaction guaranteed.

His mouth sought hers again, hot, needy, and desperate. The fire in him consumed her, sent her up in smoke. Impossibly, his arms tightened around her even more. She rose to her tiptoes, wrapping her arms around his neck. His broad shoulders were the stuff dreams were made of—strong and overbearing. Sexy. The type of thing you wanted to desperately hang onto as a man drove into you, sending you crying out in ecstasy.

His erection ground into her stomach, thick and enticingly hard, and his solid chest pushed against her swollen breasts. Arousal dampened her panties. In ten seconds, she was about ready to scramble up his body, scraping her nipples against his broad pecs and rubbing his thick length against her throbbing center.

Heat washed over her skin as her pulse quickened. The electricity sparking between them made her dizzy with a want she hadn't felt in nearly a decade. With a yearning that could only be slaked by him.

Christopher's hands slid down her sides, and he hauled her up into his arms. Her legs slid around his waist, seemingly of their own accord, and suddenly her throbbing heat was flush against his arousal, exactly where she needed him. The thin barrier of her dress and panties did little to shield her from his erection, and she gasped as he pulled her even closer.

"Which hotel is yours?" he ground out.

"One block over—" His teeth grazed her neck as he started walking, stealing her next words. She gasped as he enticingly rubbed against her with every step.

"Christopher, put me down!"

He ducked his head to her ear. "My truck's in the garage. Name and room number, or I'm taking you right there in the back of my damn pick-up."

"Oh!"

White hot lightning shot through her body as his arousal pressed exactly where she needed him. She was close, so close…. Christopher's hands slid to her thighs as she clung to him, spreading her legs even wider apart. At the rate she was going, she'd be screaming in ecstasy before they made it through the front door.

"Please," she gasped, biting her lip to keep from crying out.

Christopher ducked into a darkened doorway, pushing her back against it. They were hidden from the street, and she buried her head against his neck, muffling her cries as he thrust against her. He pushed her dress up to her hips, her lacy panties the only thing shielding her from his onslaught.

"Do you feel how hard I am for you?" His voice was so gruff it could cut steel. It was thick with desire and arousal. She was wet, desperate for him, turned on even more knowing he wanted her so badly.

She mumbled an incoherent response as she began to see stars. They weren't even undressed, and she was about to combust right here. She didn't care if the whole goddamn world could hear her. Her entire existence hinged on Christopher, on this moment. Large hands palmed her bottom, squeezing, and he ground her against him, lifting her up and down.

"Oh God," she whispered.

Heat coiled down from her center, spreading through her flushed body, nearly making her lose control. Waves of pleasure began to wash over her, threatening to pull her under. Christopher was urging her higher and higher still. When she fell, she'd never be the same again.

"Come for me, honey. Let go."

The world stopped. Spun. And she shattered, exploding into a million little pieces in Christopher's arms. She cried out his name, nearly sobbing in pleasure at her release. He held her tightly against him as she shook and rode out her explosive orgasm. After an endless crest, she finally tumbled back down from heaven, gasping. Breathlessly, she met his gaze, seeing the dark desire pooling in his eyes. Their gazes locked for heated moment, and he ducked his head, capturing her mouth again in a searing kiss.

Chapter 6

Lexi tasted sweeter than sin. Like cherries dipped in honey. Topped with whipped cream. He kissed her roughly. Possessively. Like a dying man starved for a feast. He lifted one hand to her face as he supported her weight in his other arm. His thumb skimmed over her cheek. And when her soft lips parted for him, he groaned. Fuck, she was the sweetest thing he'd ever known.

He kissed her more softly, teasing her with his lips and tongue, and felt her trembling. For him.

His tongue swept into her mouth, stroking gently against hers, and she sighed, giving in to him. His groin tightened at the tiny whimpers coming from her. Despite the slight edge she now had, nearly ten years later, she still let him take command. He'd had her coming in minutes, and they hadn't shed a single piece of clothing. Hell if that didn't make him harder than steel. His hand slid to the back of her head, tilting it further, as he claimed her mouth. Her lips were swollen and full from his kisses. Ripe. Fucking Gorgeous. His stubble grazed across her tender flesh. He'd devour her right here if she'd let him—right in the goddamn street.

He'd gone an entire lifetime without touching her, tasting her. Without taking her pleasure, making her cry out his name. Tonight she was his. She gasped, and her hands fluttered helplessly against his chest as he gently tugged on her lower lip with his teeth. He softly bit down, and then soothed the sting with his tongue. She actually moaned for him.

He was dying to feel her delicate hands trailing down his bare abdomen. To feel her knuckles grazing against his stomach…and ending up below his belt. His cock twitched at the thought of Lexi's hands on him—of her mouth sucking him deep. Fuck—he'd taught her exactly how to pleasure him. Would it still be as earth-shattering as it was in his memories? He wouldn't let himself come in her mouth though—he needed his release to be deep inside her. In the closest thing to heaven he'd ever known.

He broke their kiss and dipped his head to her ear, breathing as heavily as she was. "Take me to your hotel, Lexi. Let me love on you all night."

She whimpered, and he brushed his lips over her neck, watching her pulse jump. Her lavender scent slammed into him, and images from a lifetime ago flipped through his mind. The way she responded to him drove him fucking wild. Did she even realize the effect she had on him? How turned on he was just from being near her? Having just a taste of Lexi was not an option. His desire for her couldn't be contained. His primal urges couldn't be controlled.

"Christopher…." She sounded so helpless as she uttered his name. He wanted—needed—to make it up to her. He needed to show her with his body what he could never say in words. That she was the only woman for him—ever. Lexi was it for him. If he couldn't have her, he didn't want anyone else. He sure as hell didn't even deserve her, but he didn't think he could live with another ten years of regret weighing on his shoulders. He couldn't stand having her so close and not touching, kissing, and caressing every single inch of her body. Of not claiming her as his own once more.

"Which hotel is yours?" he asked, his voice raw with desire.

"The tallest one, a block over."

He shifted, swinging her legs up into his arms, preparing to cradle her against his chest the entire damn way.

She giggled like the girl he'd once known. "I can walk, big guy."

"Not tonight, you're not. I'm holding you close all damn night long."

Five minutes later he was shoving open the door to her hotel room, Lexi still secure in his arms. "I want you naked, beneath me," he said. His voice was gruff, unraveling. How had he survived so long without this woman at his side?

He strode across the room to the large bed, gently setting her down in front of it. Violet eyes gazed up at him, and he lifted her chin, sliding his thumb across her plump lips. There was a light rosy flush across her cheeks, either from the pleasure he'd given her moments ago or the brisk night air on their walk back. More like a full-out run. He'd beat feet with her in his arms, thankful for all those damn treks across the desert with an eighty-pound rucksack strapped to his back. A quick walk through town with a gorgeous woman—his woman—in his arms was nothing.

He needed to be atop her, inside her, and needed to hear her softly crying out his name. He'd move heaven and earth to be with her again, to make her his. Fuck, she'd just come out on the damn street from him grinding against her. He couldn't wait to feel her explode with his cock buried deep inside her silken walls, right where he belonged. The way their bodies joined together was like Lexi was made to be his. He'd screwed things up a lifetime ago, but at this moment? He'd give just about anything to make it right.

"Kiss me," she whispered, and he realized he'd been lost in his own thoughts. No need to stay there too long—Lexi was just about the only good thing about his past.

"I'll do anything you want, honey."

She rose to her tiptoes and wound her slender arms around his neck. His breathing hitched as her breasts rubbed up against his chest. He could feel her nipples harden beneath that thin sundress she had on. Blood rushed to his groin.

His hands slid between them, and he palmed her breasts, kneading and caressing as her head fell back on a soft sigh.

She needed to lose her clothes. Like yesterday.

He tugged her dress up over her head and his breath caught as he stared at the vision in black lace. Full breasts were peeking through her sexy bra, and matching panties covered her below. He fumbled, unclasping the back of her bra, then slid his fingers beneath the delicate straps. She trembled and took a sharp breath as he gently pushed them off her shoulders. Her bra fell to the ground, baring her to him. She was fucking perfect, with pale, creamy skin and rosy nipples. Even more gorgeous than he remembered. He ached for her—to feel her trembling beneath him, to feel her silken walls clamping down around his throbbing cock. To taste every square inch of her with his tongue.

He lightly squeezed her breasts, enjoying the weight of them in his hands. As they spilled over his palms, he rubbed his thumbs across her nipples, and she moaned. Long, silky black hair trailed down to her plump mounds, which were heaving up and down with each breath she took. He couldn't tear his eyes away if he wanted to. He pinched and pulled her nipples, watching them pebble beneath his fingers. He was dying to find out how wet she was for him. To see if she tasted as sweet as in his memories.

Hard as a rock, he stepped closer, a primal need to possess and pleasure her filling his chest. Throbbing in his cock. Beating in his heart.

***

Christopher's fingers sent flames licking through her body. She felt every tweak and pull of her nipples shoot straight down to her clit. He teased and tormented her, making a low, satisfied sound of approval as she gasped against him.

"Lexi, honey, I want you to come for me."

Large hands slid to her hips, and he nudged her until the backs of her legs hit the mattress and she fell onto the bed. His forearms came down at her sides, caging her in, his erection rubbed up against her soft heat, exactly where she needed him, and a second later his lips were on hers.

He kissed her thoroughly, stealing her breath, as his large body settled over her. His fingers circled her wrists, pinning her hands above her head as their tongues danced, twisted. She felt his hard-on through his pants, and heat shot through her from her head down to her toes as he pressed against her. She bucked her hips off the bed, helpless to the need he unleashed in her.

His teeth grazed across her lower lip before slowly sinking down. He tugged, nearly making her come undone.

"I need you," she gasped.

"Not yet, honey," he said, his eyes dark with arousal. "I want you burning for me."

He kissed his way down her neck, his full lips skimming over her pulse, biting her gently as she moaned. She was desperate to touch him, to grab onto his shoulders and biceps, to have anything to hold onto. His fingers tightened, holding her arms firmly in place. Hot licks of his tongue swirled across her breasts, circling around, teasing her over-sensitized nipples. She cried out for him and heard his responding guttural sound of approval.

He sucked one taut bud into his mouth, tormenting her with his tongue, before gently grazing his teeth across her stiffened peak.

"Christopher, please," she gasped.

He finally released her arms, kissing down her bare stomach as his fingers trailed up her thighs. She was wet, dripping for him. He gazed down at the black lace panties she had on and closed his eyes for a moment. "Fucking perfect," he muttered.

His knuckles grazed over her mound as he watched her, fire in his eyes.

"Please," she gasped. She felt like she was combusting, slowly burning up from the inside out. He pushed her panties aside, his thick fingers sliding through her drenched folds. He held her gaze as he touched her, seemingly mesmerized by her reaction. Fingertips fluttered against her sensitized flesh, swollen and wet for him. One thick finger sank into her molten core, and she gasped at the intimate invasion. He slid a second finger inside, stretching her for him. She moaned as he eased them in and out, slowly, much too slowly. His head dipped, and he sucked her nipple into his mouth once more.

A cascading waterfall of pleasure washed over her, making her cry out. Her hands clutched his head, raking her fingernails over his short hair. He teased her nipple with his tongue and slid his thumb in ecstasy-inducing strokes over her clit. She cried out and arched up off the bed, inadvertently pushing her breasts further up to him. He growled in approval, his thick fingers thrusting into her faster, driving her higher. His thumb circled around and around her swollen nub until the intense pleasure was too much to bear, and she cried out, a thousand shooting stars streaking across the sky.

Her waves of pleasure were endless, unstoppable. Christopher didn't let up as her body shuddered beneath him. Slowly, she fell back down to Earth, gasping for breath, Christopher's strokes finally lessening as he eased her return. Her inner walls pulsed around his fingers, and Christopher glanced up, smug male satisfaction on his face.

"Oh my God," she muttered, breathless. "I haven't—" She cut herself off, unwilling to let him know the truth.

Haven't come for another man.

Haven't come that hard—ever.

Haven't been able to get you out of my mind for nearly a decade.

"Haven't what?" he asked, softly kissing his way back up her body. His tongue trailed between her breasts, lingering, and she felt herself already growing aroused again. He trailed kisses across her collarbone, moving higher. The stubble on his face scraped against her neck, and he nibbled gently on her skin. He smelled good enough to eat—nothing but clean, delicious male. Pure Christopher.

His eyes locked with hers as he waited for her answer.

"Nothing," she said, flushing as she met his intense gaze.

"Do you moan like that for other men?" he asked, brown eyes blazing with heat.

"No," she whispered.

"You haven't been with any other man since me?" His face registered shock. His fingertips slid through her hair.

"No, I couldn't—" she cut off, looking away.

"Couldn't what?"

"Nothing." He caught her chin in his hand, gently turning her to face him. She could feel his erection pressing against her, seemingly growing harder at the thought of her never being with another man. That part wasn't true, but the idea of no other man pleasuring her seemed to make him swell with pride.

Score one for him.

"Couldn't what?" he repeated.

"Couldn't come," she said softly.

Arousal flared in his eyes. "You sure come hard for me, honey."

***

Lexi lay beneath him, flushed and sated, and he'd barely touched her. The stunning truth was practically unbelievable—ten damn years had gone by, and no other man could get her off? Fucking idiots. The dudes she'd been with must have been complete imbeciles, because she shot off like a firecracker whenever he touched her. He could spend hours tracing over her skin with his fingertips, swirling his tongue over her soft curves, driving his shaft into her sweet folds. And she didn't respond to anyone but him?

Holy hell.

Male pride surged through him. He felt strong, invincible, capable of taking on the whole world. He'd been a fucking fool to ever run from her.

And he was the damn luckiest man on Earth to have run into her tonight.

Gently, he slipped his hands inside those lacy black panties, adrenaline surging through him at her intake of breath. His knuckles grazed over her flat stomach for a moment before he finally slid the scrap of lace down her shapely legs. As he gazed back up at Lexi, her flushed cheeks, swollen breasts, and rosy nipples nearly took his breath away. And that patch of dark hair down below was covering the sweetest spot of all. He was dying to sink deep inside her velvety channel, sending them both to heaven.

He ripped off his shirt, liquid heat pooling inside him as her eyes trailed over his abdomen. He kept in good shape and knew women always appreciated his muscular torso, but having Lexi look at him that way was hotter than hell.

"Well, damn," she said.

Christopher chuffed out a laugh. Hell if it didn't make him feel ten feet tall having Lexi's eyes run over him like that. To have her look at him the way she once did made him prouder than damn near anything. Her approval meant everything to him—nothing else mattered. How he'd screwed it up so badly was a damn mystery. He was young and stupid then— nothing but a fool.

He toed off his boots, and a second later tugged down his pants and boxer briefs. His erection sprang out, and he throbbed as he watched Lexi lick her lips. He didn't have enough control to let her take him in her mouth tonight. He was hanging on the edge as it was, about to explode just from being with her.

He bent over her supple body, his arousal pushing up against her slick folds, and kissed her gently. She whimpered as he gently probed her mouth with his tongue. She writhed beneath him, her heat rubbing up against his swollen cock and driving him damn near insane. "Are you still on the pill?" he asked between soft kisses. He'd never gone bare for any women but her. He'd wear a condom if she wanted, but it would just fucking kill him. He needed her trust.

"Uh-huh," she panted, gently bucking her hips against him.

"I'll wear a condom if you want, but I promise I'm clean, honey. The only woman I've ever gone without is you."

Her cheeks heated, and he searched her violet eyes. Why the hell that should embarrass her, he didn't have a fucking clue. The fact that she'd been inexperienced when they first met just made him that much damn harder for her. Just made her that much sweeter. Add in the revelation that he'd been the only man to ever steal her pleasure and he was damn near flying into the stratosphere.

For a man who'd been relatively on his own his entire life, taking care of Lexi and making her happy was the best thing he'd ever known. Maybe the greatest thing he'd ever done. She was the only future he'd wanted, and the fact that he'd ruined it lay heavily on his chest. He'd screwed it up, but there wasn't a day that went by that her violet eyes and innocent smile didn't haunt his dreams.

He ducked his head and stole another kiss, nudging his erection against her swollen clit. She gasped and opened her legs further to him, sending him a clear invitation to take it all the way home. Positioning himself, he eased into her opening, slowly edging the swollen head of his shaft into her tight heat. He grit his teeth, holding back as he slid in inch by painstaking inch. He needed to go slow, to make it good for her, too.

He laced his fingers with hers, his own hands rough and calloused compared to her smooth, creamy skin. He held her arms up above her head, pinning them to the mattress. She clutched onto his hands desperately as her walls clenched down around him, she was already so wound up. Slowly, he pulled out and pushed back in, stretching her, making her his. Lexi moaned beneath him as he gently thrust, and he kissed her again, stealing her breath. Having her supple body beneath him, exactly where she belonged, was a goddamn dream.

He adjusted his position, hitting that secret spot inside that drove her absolutely wild. She cried out, trying to move away from the intense pleasure, but he had her pinned to the mattress. She ground her hips against his, moving in perfect sync with him. Their bodies weren't two separate entities anymore; they were one.

The little mewls and whimpers coming from her lips were captured by his mouth, hot over hers. Her inner walls pulsed, milking his throbbing cock, and male pride surged through him as he drove her toward ecstasy.

Come for me, honey.

Only for me.

He wanted to roar in approval at satisfying his woman. The need to care for and protect a woman was engrained in his DNA. The desire to sate her in the bedroom was just as strong. Christopher took care of what was his—in any and every way imaginable. She was his to satisfy, and he wanted to make sure she knew it down to her very soul.

He thrust harder, deeper, loving her little gasps. He was throbbing, desperate for release, but not without taking her pleasure first. Within seconds she was crying out, bucking beneath him. She screamed as her body arched up against his, her breasts pushing against his chest, her pussy gripping him like a vise. His balls tightened, and he pumped into her again, releasing deep inside Lexi as he shouted her name.

Shockwaves coursed through his body, a million nights without her worth every lonely minute for their connection tonight. Fucking hell. He glanced down at her, those innocent violet eyes on him. Her body was coated in a light sheen of sweat, her cheeks flushed, her hair tousled and sexy as fuck. He released his grip on her delicate hands, rolling them both to the side, still buried deep inside his woman. He hitched Lexi's leg up over his hip and then collected her tightly in his arms, listening to the soft sounds of her breathing.

"Are you okay?"

"Um…yeah. Way better than okay."

Christopher chuckled, and kissed her cherry lips. He was already growing hard again, buried balls deep inside her, needing to take her again.

Her eyes grew wide, and his hand slid to her ass, pulling her impossibly closer. She was soft and warm, somehow still innocent despite the passage of time, and still completely gorgeous with bombshell curves that would put a supermodel to shame. He didn't know what he'd done to deserve a night in Lexi's arms, but hell if he never wanted it to end. He never wanted another woman in his bed again. He sure as hell never wanted Lexi being kissed, touched, or pleasured by another man. He'd found what he'd lost all those years ago, and nothing—no one—would take her away.

Christopher rolled to his back, pulling Lexi along with him. Dark hair cascaded down, teasing the ample curves of her breasts and rosy nipples. He wanted to run his fingers through her smooth locks, kiss and suck on those gorgeous tits, and fuck her into oblivion.

Her thighs settled on either side of his, so soft against his own hard muscles, and he groaned as she sank further down, completely impaled by him.

He thrust up into her, grinding himself against her

clit, and his name fell softly from her lips. Gripping her curvy hips, he thrust again, watching her eyes slide shut as her head fell back. He held her to him, taking all control of their lovemaking, and gave her exactly what she needed. Gorgeous breasts bounced up and down, her silken walls tightened around his shaft, but it was the expression on her face that nearly made him come undone—pure, unadulterated bliss, brought on by him.

Adrenaline and heat surged through him as the need to sate her took over. He needed her coming on his cock, breathing his name, and collapsing into his arms. He urged her higher and higher, bucking beneath her, sending her straight toward oblivion.

"Christopher," she gasped.

He pulled her down hard as he thrust up again, and she shattered, crying out once more in ecstasy. His cock hardened, and his seed exploded inside her, marking her, claiming her as his.

"Oh God," she cried out, finally meeting his eyes. "Christopher…."

His name on her lips was the sweetest damn sound he'd ever heard.

Chapter 7

Christopher stretched and rolled over in bed the next morning, his body exhausted. He'd kept Lexi up practically all goddamn night, and he wasn't twenty-four anymore. His body was feeling the lack of shut-eye. All night lovemaking sessions weren't something he'd enjoyed the pleasure of in a damn long time. Hell if time and age weren't catching up with him. That and the fact that there was only one woman he needed above all others.

He slid one hand across the bed, wondering where she'd disappeared to, and realized the sheets beside him were cold. Sitting up, his eyes fell on a scrap of paper next to him on the wooden nightstand.

Big meeting this a.m. See you around. -Lexi

Christopher scanned over the note for the third time, clenching his jaw. See you around? That sentiment might sit better with him if it was from an acquaintance he barely knew, not the woman he'd just spent the night making love to. And it sure as hell didn't bode well coming from Lexi. How the hell had she snuck out? He was a goddamned SEAL, trained to be attuned to his surroundings, to be on guard at all times. Yet somehow the woman he'd slept with had slipped out of the bed they'd shared—out of his arms for fuck's sake—and simply left?

Sonofabitch.

Christopher scrubbed his hand over his face, muttering in disbelief. That note sure as shit didn't sound too promising. It wasn't exactly covered in little hearts and smiley faces or any of that other flowery stuff woman loved. Presumably if she was okay with the way the night had ended—with them making love until nearly dawn—she'd have stuck around. Maybe even been up for a morning tumble between the sheets.

He stood, the tangled sheets falling to the ground, and snatched his boxer briefs from the floor. Lexi's lavender scent was all over his skin, and his cock twitched at the memories of her soft and warm body beneath him.

He'd chased after her last night wanting to explain everything—to come clean on the reason he'd freaked out on her back in Coronado. To explain why he'd panicked at the idea of becoming a dad. Although Lexi knew his own father had left him, she didn't know the half of the shit he'd dealt with as a kid. Of his fear of turning out just like his old man. Christopher had never planned to be a father, and the moment Lexi said she was pregnant, he'd literally frozen in fear. What were the stages of grief? Denial, anger, and finally acceptance?

He'd driven around until dawn all those years ago,

finally realizing he'd do whatever it took to protect Lexi and his child. That he had more honor and integrity in him at age twenty-four than his dad had his entire life. Christopher would never harm a woman, and he sure as hell would never hurt an innocent child.

His revelations were too little too late. Lexi had slammed the door in his face, and until she'd walked into Anchors, it was the last time they'd spoken. One of her roommates had shown up a week after they'd broken up, telling him the pregnancy scare had been a false alarm. Oh yeah, and that Lexi was long gone.

Regret tore through his chest at never going after her.

He dressed quickly, alone in her empty hotel room. His shucked on his tee shirt, memories of Lexi desperately clutching it last night churning in his mind. His eyes swept the room. Her purse was gone, but her suitcase was propped open on the dresser. Not that he'd really expected her to run out on the job. Lexi had been a whip-smart computer sciences students back in California, the only female intern in a group of male computer security trainees. She'd blasted past those guys, coming out in the top of her classes. He'd been prouder than hell of her and upset beyond belief that she'd left in the middle of her college career because of him. Presumably she'd finished her degree somewhere on the East Coast, eventually working her way up the ranks in the Pentagon.

And now their first encounter after a night of unbridled passion would be at a damn IT security briefing on base? Hell. He hadn't even told her that he'd be there. She'd go ballistic when she saw him sitting in on the meeting. There hadn't exactly been time for a lot of conversation in between making love all night long. And she sure hadn't given him a chance to get in a word this morning.

She'd cut and run, leaving him alone with his regrets.

He needed a good run to clear his head. To figure out his game plan. If he thought she was angry to unexpectedly see him last night at Anchors, she was going to be livid that he was sitting in on her meeting this morning. No way would she expect a SEAL sitting in with the network security staff, but hell if he wasn't as good as her at hacking into systems unbeknownst and undetected. If his CO needed him there, he was there. Christopher put the mission first, and even a woman like Lexi wasn't enough to change that. If she didn't want him there, that was too damn bad. It's not like she was running the place.

Stopping the attempted hacks into the secure systems was mission critical. The Top Secret military information stored on their servers couldn't ever be leaked into the wrong hands. And come hell or high water, he was coming clean with her about his past. Today.

After a quick five miles, Christopher showered and changed in the locker room on base. His muscles tensed at the memory of moving over Lexi last night. Pinning her down beneath him had damn near driven him out of his mind. She was soft and sweet. Enticing. Claiming her as his years ago was the smartest damn thing he'd ever done. How he'd fucked that up was beyond all reason.

His run had done little to assuage the adrenaline and guilt racking through him. He was strung tight, ready to snap at any second. The tension at the thought of seeing her again coursed through his body. A long run and hot shower seemed like the only reasonable way to start his day. No doubt waking alone in a woman's hotel room would leave a man riddled with uneasy thoughts churning through his mind.

The sludge that passed for coffee in the mess hall did little to make up for his lack of shut-eye. The high he'd gotten from running earlier hadn't lasted thanks to his passion-fueled night. He wasn't a fancy coffee kind of man, but at the moment, he'd kill for a couple shots of espresso. Just so he could think clearly and get his damn head on straight.

He tensed as he heard voices, and a second later, his SEAL team leader Patrick strode into the locker room, grabbing his gear for their day's training. "I heard you're sitting in on the computer hacking briefing this a.m.," Patrick said, stuffing his bag in his locker.

"Yeah, the CO wants me there, I figure he owes somebody a favor, roping me into this."

Patrick nodded. "We're drilling out on the water. It'll be Evan's first time out since he's been back."

"It'll be good for him to get back out there with the team. I wouldn't mind being out there myself this morning."

Patrick chuffed out a laugh. "Mike said your ex is the hotshot specialist from the Pentagon?"

"Something like that," Christopher muttered.

"You're screwed, man. Nothing's worse than a woman scorned. Especially one who's had years to stew over it."

"Sonofabith."

"What the hell did you do to her?"

"Doesn't matter. We were practically just kids then."

Patrick raised his eyebrows.

Mike swung open the door to the locker room, dropping his bag full of gear on the ground. He grinned as he caught sight of them. "All right lover boy, how was she?"

Christopher clenched his fists. "None of your goddamn business."

Mike laughed. "Hell, I figure any woman that has your lousy ass chasing her down the block must be pretty damn fine."

"Fuck you," Christopher spat out, slamming his locker door shut.

Patrick's cool blue gaze slid to him. "Just don't let a woman get in the way of the mission," he said, throwing Christopher's words from months earlier back at him. Their SEAL team had gotten sent out on an op right after the confrontation with Rebecca's stalker and subsequent argument between Patrick and Rebecca. Patrick had been broken up over it, and Christopher had told him to keep his head in the game.

Not that he and Lexi were anything remotely like Patrick and Rebecca.

"Hell. You and Rebecca were together when I said that. This is old news—a decade old. That ship has sailed."

"Right. That's why you're always bitching about your ex from California. Because you're over her," Mike laughed.

"Both of you can go to hell," Christopher muttered.

"You're welcome," Patrick smirked, starting to walk away.

"Already on my way," Mike quipped.

Christopher stalked out of the locker room, biting out a curse. He should've known his advice to Patrick all those months ago would come back to bite him in the ass. Since when was he a goddamn expert on relationships? Lexi wouldn't get in the way of anything. She wasn't even on his radar enough to get in the way. Maybe their night together was just him blowing off some steam, scratching an itch that had been bothering him for a decade. That shit didn't mean anything. It sure the fuck didn't mean he couldn't do his job. Jesus.

He stormed down the hall, clenching his fists. Maybe they could solve this shit today and Lexi would be on her way back to her office at the Pentagon by nightfall. She'd walk out of his life, and he'd move on. Again.

Fucking hell.

Maybe if he didn't have to worry about being near her he could actually breathe again. Maybe his pulse would stop pounding and his body wouldn't be on full-blown alert. His chest clenched just thinking about sitting across the table from her all morning long. He'd gone years, years, without seeing her, and now he'd finally be able to feast his eyes on her for hours on end?

Hell.

How was he supposed to look and not touch when he'd just spent an entire night with her wrapped around him? How was he supposed to play it cool when hours ago his cock had been buried so deeply in her tight heat he barely knew where he stopped and she began?

He didn't need a cup of coffee to clear his head, he needed a whole damn pot. And quite possibly a cold shower. Jesus.

Chapter 8

Lexi sank into a chair in the conference room, glancing at the clock on the wall. Fifteen minutes until go time. She'd give a brief rundown of what she'd already presented yesterday to the top brass and then get into the nitty-gritty, working with the IT staff to pinpoint the source of the attempted hacking. A day spent looking at lines of code and tracking down IP addresses that likely jumped all over the world might yield minimal results. They'd have to dig deeper and stop this before it became a political fiasco. No one wanted sensitive, Top Secret military information getting into the wrong hands.

She groaned.

It was going to be a freaking long day.

Downing the last of the large black coffee she'd picked up on her drive over, she tossed the empty cup into the trash can. She needed about five more of those with the lack of sleep she'd gotten last night.

Running into Christopher at Anchors had left her mind spinning in circles, and having him chase her down and haul her back to her hotel room had sent her reeling. When he'd spun her around on the sidewalk, capturing her in a kiss, suddenly she'd been nineteen again, smitten with the hunky Navy SEAL.

At least she'd be stuck in the conference and server rooms all day—less chance of running into Christopher or any of his SEAL buddies. If anything, the man was even more attuned to her body than years ago. Be it experience, age, or just their earth-shattering connection, he'd sent her flying higher than ever before. Last night had felt good—too good. With his hot lips on hers and thick length stroking her inside, she'd barely been able to breathe. She didn't want to pick up where they'd left off years ago; she didn't need a man like him in her life. Not someone who overwhelmed her, consumed her, and then broke her damn heart.

Maybe her mind had short-circuited last night, but if she saw him again while she was in town, she'd steer clear. No sense in letting him think they were going for round two or three. One night was all her heart could handle with Christopher. The sex had been downright spectacular, maybe even the type of stuff songs were written about, but she'd have suffice with just the memories.

If she fell for him again, she'd never recover.

Stifling a yawn, she rose from her chair. The coffee they served on base was likely worthless. Maybe she'd hit up a vending machine for a can of soda before the briefing started. Digging through her purse for some change, she grabbed a few quarters and headed for the door. She needed more caffeine in her veins to help her think straight. Glancing back at the clock again, she nearly smacked right into Christopher, his large, broad frame taking up way too much space in the doorway. Making her far too aware of him. She jumped back, his masculine, clean scent hanging in the air between them, and gasped, both from nearly colliding with him and from the way his closeness sent shivers snaking down her spine.

"Lexi," he ground out, not seeming surprised in the least to see her.

That made one of them.

His large hands clasped her shoulders, steadying her, and the angry words she had ready for him melted away as heat coursed through her body. The weight of them had her imagining all sorts of things she shouldn't—like Christopher's powerful body atop of hers as he pinned her down, her wrists in his grasp. Like the two of them making love until practically dawn, with her whimpering, begging him for release. He'd made her come so many times her head had been swimming when she'd finally drifted off into a deep slumber. It was amazing she was even functioning at all this morning after a night like that. She was still deliciously sore from their night of lovemaking, and she didn't need to see him as a reminder. She sure the hell didn't need to start her briefing both angry and aroused.

His eyes sparked with heat, and electricity surged between them. She felt small compared to his massive size, sheltered, as she always had when he was near. He was big. Dominant. Fully in control. He didn't move his hands from her shoulders, and her heartbeat sped up. For a seemingly innocent gesture, her body was suddenly on high alert.

A beat passed as their eyes locked, and her lips slightly parted. His head seemed to move a fraction of an inch closer to her, and her gaze shifted to his full male lips. Kissing Christopher had always been nearly as fantastic as having sex—or maybe it was just the promises his kisses held of what was to come. The heat of them was enough to keep her warm many a cold winter night.

Christopher finally groaned and released her, stepping back. She shakily smoothed her hands over her skirt, as if that would somehow calm her frayed nerves. He looked slightly rattled himself.

"What are you doing here?" she asked, her eyebrows narrowing in confusion.

Just about the only damn reason she'd come to base this morning and not high-tailed it back to the Pentagon was knowing she'd be nowhere near Christopher or any of the SEALs. She'd snuck out of her hotel room before he was up and hunkered down in an empty conference room just to avoid exactly that.

"My CO asked me to sit in on the meeting."

"He asked you to help with the attempted hacks?"

Christopher smirked. "Does that surprise you?"

"Hell yes it surprises me. I'm supposed to meet with the IT staff today, not a freaking Navy SEAL."

"You never used to have a problem with my being a SEAL if memory serves right," he said, his voice gruff.

"We never worked together before," she snapped.

"We were pretty damn good together last night." He raised his eyebrows.

Fuming, she moved past him, the skin on her bare arm electrifying as she brushed against his shirtsleeve.

Holy crap. She was about to go up in flames just from that innocent touch. She marched down the hallway, her blood boiling. Not only would she have to be on base with Christopher, but they'd be sitting in the same room? Perfect. She could really use the distraction of a past lover to keep her mind on her work. Shit. Shit. Shit.

She stopped when she reached a dead end and turned around, puzzled. Weren't the vending machines this way?

Christopher was still standing in the doorway of the conference room, arms crossed against his chest, watching her with an amused expression on his face. "Having second thoughts about running off?"

"I'm not running off; I'm looking for the damn vending machines."

He cocked his head in the opposite direction, a smile playing on his lips.

The hell with him.

She let out an exasperated sigh and stormed back down the hall. She felt like she was entering the lion's den with the way Christopher's predatory gaze swept over her. Why had she worn her impossibly high heels again? His eyes slid up her legs, and she could practically feel them burning into her skin. Her nipples tightened, and arousal pooled at her center.

He seemed entranced watching the way her hips swished back and forth in the slim pencil skirt she had on. She might as well be prancing around for him in her lingerie or something with the heated look in his eyes. Not that she pranced around for any man.

His lips parted slightly as his gaze fell on her chest, and she glared at him. No other man would openly ogle her this way at the office. So what if they had a history together? She didn't need his lust-filled gaze staring at her all morning.

"Keep it in your pants," she snapped as she walked by him.

He looked momentarily startled and then flashed her a grin.

"Whatever you say, honey."

Heat burned through her. When Christopher used to call her 'honey,' it was sweet. Intimate. Now he said it almost tauntingly, like she was just any random chick he'd banged. Like they weren't on base with eyes and ears everywhere. She glared at him.

"Take a left up there. Vending machines are on the right," he called out.

She flipped him off before she rounded the corner, and she could hear his deep laughter all the way down the hall. It was the first time she'd heard him laugh since seeing him again, and something stirred deep inside her. Something unwelcome and unwanted.

This was going to be the freaking longest day of her life. She wasn't sure which was more infuriating— having Christopher stare at her like that after all these years, like she was his, or the way her damn body betrayed her, responding to him in a way it wouldn't—couldn't— for anyone else.

She slid two quarters into the machine and punched her selection. The machine rumbled as the can of soda tumbled down. It remained there, waiting for her to retrieve it, as the hair on the back of her neck stood up and goosebumps spread over her flesh. Christopher's warmth seeped into her as he stopped behind her, his large body looming over hers. His scent was so masculine and enticing, it was all she could do not to turn around and bury her face in his neck.

Christopher stood so close that if she bent over to pick up her soda, her ass would brush against his groin. Probably exactly what he wanted, she thought with a smirk. She was trapped between him and the humming vending machine, her own body humming with a different kind of vibration. The way that man got to her was unnerving. He wasn't even touching her, but she was unable to move. Trapped by his dominance and power.

"Why'd you run out on me this morning?" he asked, his voice low and smooth.

"I didn't run out; you knew exactly where to find me."

He bent down, his lips hovering at her ear, "I was hoping to hear you begging for me again."

She spun around and shoved at his immobile chest. "Don't be an asshole."

He nailed her with a gaze. "We need to talk."

"Like hell we do." Anger coursed through her. This was exactly what she'd expected to happen this morning—Christopher to just assume they'd spend another night together, like it was no big deal. She'd given in to him last night, caving in to what her body had yearned for, but that was a one-time occurrence. Nothing good could come from spending another night with him. Not when the ending had already been written.

"I'm sorry."

Unwelcome tears filled her eyes. "You're about nine years too late."

Christopher clenched his jaw and swallowed, his Adam's apple bobbing. "Walking out on you was the biggest fucking mistake of my life."

"I guess we all have to learn to live with regret," she retorted, brushing past him as she walked away. Her heels clicked as she rushed down the empty corridor, and without even looking back, she knew Christopher was still exactly where she'd left him. The pain etched on his face was almost unbearable. It was the same hurt she'd locked away in her own heart.

She was halfway down the hall when she realized she'd forgotten her damn soda.

***

Lexi scanned over the IP addresses again late that afternoon, hunched over a work station in the server room. After a one-hour briefing this morning, explaining to the IT staff what she'd already covered with the higher ups yesterday, they'd moved out of the stuffy conference room and gotten down to business.

To her relief—and with only a slight twinge of disappointment—Christopher had spoken to some of the IT staff and taken off after the meeting. It was for the best. His eyes boring into hers as she'd addressed the room had caused her to stumble over her words at one point—and she never floundered when speaking in front of a crowd. Hell, she dealt with the top brass at the Pentagon daily. And she couldn't handle conducting a meeting with her ex in the room? She was losing her edge around him.

He'd been professional, at least. Respectful even. Nodding in agreement at points, looking impressed when she gave a brief rundown of her background to the others. Having an outsider sent in from the

Pentagon—and a woman at that—didn't always go well in a male-dominated environment. No one had so much as even looked at her the wrong way this morning, let alone implied that a woman wasn't up to the task. Thank God for that. She'd spent enough time dealing with assholes as she'd moved up the career ladder.

She punched a few buttons on the computer screen, the new IP addresses she was tracing popping up on a map of the world. Another click, and lines connected the myriad addresses that jumped across the globe, tracing a path. She set down her can of diet soda and glanced at the stack of papers she'd printed out. The hackers had covered their tracks well, routing themselves through servers in countries scattered across the planet. Their trail was difficult to follow. Impossible to trace. And exactly what they'd intended.

"Making any progress?" Captain Edwards, a hardened career Navy man and head of the network security staff on base, poked his head into the server room where Lexi was working with some of the other techs. He'd checked in twice earlier and seemed eager for progress to be made on the attempted hacks. As head of the network security team, no doubt his ass was on the line. He likely was unhappy that Lexi had been pulled into the mess. The Navy liked to handle their own issues, without officials from the Pentagon being sent down to intervene and report back to Washington. Captain Edwards had been polite but cool to Lexi, and the stormy look in his eyes each time they crossed paths made her jumpy and on edge. Nothing like trying to concentrate and focus on your work when someone was watching you like a hawk.

More like a cobra, she thought. He seemed ready to strike at any moment.

"We'll get there," Lexi promised.

"Let me know if you need anything," he said, appraising her.

"Of course," she said.

He nodded curtly and left. She exchanged glances with one of the military men she'd been working with all afternoon.

"Is he always such a hard ass?'

"That was nothing," the guy said, chuckling. "He's been nothing but civilized to you."

"I can't wait to catch him on bad day," she muttered.

They'd given her room to take the lead on this investigation, but she needed to get some results. She'd played around with the idea of upping the network security, making it impossible for anyone to ever find their servers at Little Creek, let alone attempt to hack into them again. Or she could set up a honey pot—a trove of false information that would be utterly irresistible to the hackers. After they downloaded the falsified files, a Trojan horse virus would infiltrate their systems, leaving them open to an attack. And one hundred percent traceable by Lexi.

She wished she had a clue as to who was after the information stored on the classified databases. If it was just some dumb college kids fooling around, seeing what they could hack into, they'd be prosecuted, but it wouldn't be worth setting up the dummy data and honey pot. If, on the other hand, it was indeed foreign nationals or some other adversary after Top Secret government data, then it had to be dealt with using the fullest extent of her capabilities.

She straightened her stack of papers and shoved them into her briefcase. The jumble of IP addresses wasn't classified information, and she'd cull through them later on back at the hotel, seeing if she could glean anything new. The IT night shift on base would search through some of the code they'd been able to pull from one attempted penetration, seeing if the hackers had left any inadvertent clues. And after a couple of hours of shut-eye, they'd reconvene at oh-seven-hundred.

Eight hours spent analyzing data, and they weren't any closer to finding the culprit than when they'd started this morning. Her chances of returning to Arlington on Friday were looking slimmer and slimmer.

She called Kenley as she climbed into her SUV, leaving the phone on speaker as she started the engine. "How was the game last night?" AC cranked up, windows cranked down. She was ready to roll.

"Nat's won, Yankees lost."

Lexi laughed. "You didn't take Cassidy to the game, did you? She would've been pissed."

"Nope. Just me, myself, and I. How are things at Little Creek?"

"Disastrous," she said.

"You can't solve the computer mumbo jumbo?"

Lexi rolled her eyes. "Of course I'll figure that out—eventually. It's more the entire male species that's causing me problems."

"You met a guy?"

"Just a blast from the past." More like a freaking brick wall.

"Wait—you mean the guy you ran clear across the country from?"

"The very one."

"Holy shit."

Lexi laughed. Nearly a decade of friendship, and she'd never once heard Kenley utter a single swear word. "Now imagine how I feel."

"That's insane."

"That it is. Anyway, I'm not sure if I'll be back by the weekend, either. The computer 'mumbo jumbo' as you so eloquently put it is major. I many have to bail on you and Cassidy for girl's night."

"Sure you not just busy getting hot and heavy with the ex?" Kenley teased.

"I'm up to my eyeballs in work. Besides, he's a complete ass," Lexi said, choosing to leave out that fact that she'd slept with an ex. Perfect. Now she was lying to her best friend, sleeping with the enemy, and not any closer to tracking down the hackers than she had been this morning. What a catastrophe of a day.

"Hmmm. Maybe Cassidy and I can take a trip down to the beach for the weekend. You'll have some free time, right?"

Lexi smiled. "Yeah, definitely. You want to crash at my hotel?" She pulled onto Atlantic Avenue, already feeling lighter with the salty air blowing in through her open windows.

"If Cassidy comes, too, we'll probably just crash at the condo. We'll come by though."

"Awesome. Let me know what you guys decide."

"Sure thing. Talk to you soon? I've got to wrap up some stuff at the office."

"Sounds good. Bye, hun."

"Bye."

She pushed "end" and tossed her phone onto the passenger seat. She'd left base without another confrontation with a frustrating Navy SEAL. Her best friends may turn her extended business trip into a beach weekend. The day was suddenly looking up.

Chapter 9

Christopher pulled out of the parking lot on base, trailing behind Lexi at a safe distance. He'd wanted to nab her before she left for the day, but the drills he'd joined his SEAL team for out on the water had taken longer than he'd expected. He'd sprinted out to his car just in time to see her pulling away. Maybe it was for the best, because what he had to say needed to be done in private. Far from the guys on his SEAL team, who'd been ribbing him about the fuck-up at Anchors last night. Lexi storming out on him was now permanently engrained in all of their memories. Hell.

He followed her for ten minutes, his mind flashing back to tailing Rebecca all those months ago during the stalker incident. Lexi didn't seem to have the first clue that he was hot on her tail, and his gut churned. Maybe after they spoke about the mistakes that had haunted him for a decade, he'd teach her some basic safety precautions. A single woman couldn't be too careful.

She pulled into a parking garage off Atlantic Avenue, across the street from a long strip of hotels. He signaled and turned in behind her. Christopher's hands gripped the steering wheel as she chose the spot in the far corner. Granted, there weren't any other open spaces left on this level. He'd tell her to use the valet at her hotel so she wasn't walking around alone in parking garages all the time. Not that she was his concern anymore, but hell. The thought of something happening to her left a tightening in his chest that he didn't want to examine too closely.

She was a big girl. A grown woman. Somehow she'd survived the past nine years without him. Fuck. There'd probably been other men, other boyfriends around. Maybe she wasn't married, but she'd never said she was alone. The thought of another man's hands on Lexi made his blood boil. Seeing her again after all this time sent his brain short-circuiting, filling him with primal urges to make her his again. So what if he'd screwed up a decade ago. He wasn't some young kid anymore, he was a man. And hell if he wouldn't protect and defend those he cared about.

Lexi was mad at him, but hell. If he had to get down on his knees and fucking grovel, he wasn't above doing so. Just for a damn chance to make the ache in his heart go away—to let her know despite everything, no matter what happened, she was the one thing he cared about in his life. He'd screwed it up royally, but if he had the tiniest shot at making things right, he'd do it in a heartbeat.

She remained in her SUV as he pulled past, driving up the ramp to the next level. His pulse pounded as he realized this level was also full. If he followed her all the way here only to lose sight of her in the damn parking garage, he was going to lose his shit. No fucking way would she let him in her hotel room. Not after she'd snuck out this morning.

He drummed his fingers on the steering wheel, turning up another level. Christ. He was about ready to leave his pick-up double-parked while he chased her down. Finally, he saw a car up ahead backing out, and he sped up, waiting for their spot. It took them several minutes to make an easy maneuver out of the parking spot, and he half considered jumping out of his truck and offering to back it out for them.

At this point, Lexi was probably already long gone.

Finally they pulled away, leaving him the precious empty space. He easily pulled his pick-up into the spot and jumped out, running to the stairs in the corner. Lexi was on the ground level, and maybe if he sprinted down he could spot her on the street. He needed to find his girl.

***

Lexi grabbed her briefcase from the passenger seat and climbed out of her SUV. She clicked the remote, setting the alarm, and walked through the lower level of the garage. The place was filled with cars, but oddly enough, there were no other people around. The clicking of her heels on the pavement was the only sound, aside from the street noise drifting in, giving the garage an eerily deserted feel. The bass from a stereo thumped loudly as a car sat at a light, and a moment later, the engine accelerated as it drove off. She wrinkled her nose in disgust as exhaust filled the air.

A large black SUV appeared in the entrance of the garage, its headlights flicking on as it pulled into the darkened structure. She held a hand to her eyes, shielding them from the brightness. Why the hell were they just sitting there, lights beaming right at her?

She sighed and turned toward the stairwell. There was an exit to the street there, too. She'd go out that door and cross Atlantic Avenue to her hotel. No biggie.

The SUV pulled forward as she reached for the handle to the stairwell, stopping only a few feet from where she stood. Uneasiness washed over her. An entire parking garage, and they stopped beside her?

"Excuse me!" a man's deep, authoritative voice rang out.

A tinted window in the rear of the vehicle unrolled, and she saw the slimy guy in a suit that had been watching her last night. Dark hair slicked back, clean shaven, and still wearing sunglasses even though they were in a garage so dark that the driver had turned on his headlights.

A shiver raced down her spine.

It wasn't like he was some random thug off the street. He was staying in an oceanfront resort. She was already at the stairway of the parking garage, only feet from the exit. It's not like he'd rob her or rape her in broad daylight, within spitting distance from traffic on the street.

Would he?

She pulled the handle of the door to the stairwell, surprised to hear someone running down the steps. Someone big, judging from the loud thumping. They were only one level above her. Holy shit. Were there more than just the guys in the vehicle? What the hell did they want with her?

Her heart hammered in her chest, and she frantically looked around. They were on street level. She could run between the parked cars and climb over the concrete wall facing Atlantic Avenue. She'd land in a bunch of bushes, but that would be a hell of a lot better than being trapped in the stairs with Rambo or being pulled into the black SUV, occupants unknown.

She had to get the hell out of here. She released the handle, the large, heavy door beginning to swing shut. She'd rather chance running through the parking garage than risk the unknown.

"Excuse me!" the man from the SUV called out again. The backdoor opened.

She turned away, clutching her briefcase in both hands. If someone came after her, she'd have to use it as a weapon.

"Sorry, I'm late!" she shouted. Would someone on the street even hear her if she screamed?

The pounding down the stairs came faster as the man neared the bottom.

"Lexi?"

She halted, a mixture of relief and surprise washing over her. That sounded like...Christopher? What the hell was he doing here? A day ago, he was the last man on earth she would to run into, but at this moment, she'd never been so happy to hear his voice in her life.

She spun back toward the stairwell as the backdoor to the SUV slammed shut, and it quickly backed out of the garage, tires squealing as they took off. She stared after them in shock as Christopher came pushing through the door. She looked over at him, wide-eyed, clutching her briefcase to her chest.

"Shit, did I scare you?" he asked, rushing to her side. "You're white as a ghost."

She lowered her briefcase with trembling hands.

"Lexi," he said, his voice a low rumble. She met his concerned gaze, and Christopher took her briefcase from her in one large hand, gently lifting his other hand to her cheek. Without thinking, she relaxed into his warmth. This was crazy. For all she knew, those guys were asking her for directions or something. But why'd they take off when they heard Christopher coming? And what was he doing here anyway?

She unsteadily stepped back from his searing touch, wobbling in her heels. She blinked. The ground spun beneath her.

His muscular arm wrapped around her waist, pulling her back, holding her close to his side. He still gripped her briefcase, not even bothering to use the handle. Geez, his hands were massive. Something sparked inside of her at the memory of them trailing across her skin. She tried to pull away, to stop the onslaught of unwelcome memories, but he held her close.

Christopher was a wall of rigid muscle beside her. His clean, masculine scent surrounded her, and the warmth from his frame seeped into her as he tucked her against his side, making her feel safe, secure. Her body relaxed into him, her breathing uneven. The adrenaline pumping through her was because of her fright. It had nothing to do with the hard-edged SEAL holding her close.

"Lexi, you're shaking." He bent and set her

briefcase on the ground before turning her to face him, his sure hands gripping her waist. The weight of them sent her reeling, her head spinning. She'd fall over if Christopher wasn't holding her up.

"Did something happen?" he asked. Gentle brown eyes searched hers.

"Those guys—I thought—"

"What guys?" His brow furrowed.

"There was a car, right before you got here. An SUV. I saw this creepy guy watching me last night at my hotel. And he was here. Now." She shook her head, trying to clear her disjointed thoughts. Christopher watched her hair swish back and forth before once again searching her face. She wasn't even speaking coherently, just rambling like some lunatic.

"Lexi." His voice was soothing. Quiet.

She met his gaze and swallowed.

"Tell me what happened. Should I call the police?" Anger sparked in his eyes. God, he'd probably chase after them himself if she let him. Christopher had always been one of those protective, alpha males. He was cocky and arrogant with the goods to back it up. But he was also fiercely protective of those he cared about—or was most of the time, she thought bitterly, recalling the way it had ended between them years ago.

She let out a shaky breath, her resolve strengthening. "Just forget it. I can take care of myself."

"Hell, Lexi," he ground out. "I know you're still mad at me. But so help me God, tell me what the fuck just happened. If someone is trying to hurt you, I'll rip their goddamn heart out."

The aggressiveness in his voice startled her.

Calmed her. Just because she was mad at Christopher her ex-boyfriend didn't mean Christopher the Navy SEAL wouldn't protect her. Her eyelids slid shut, and she took a deep breath. He was watching her closely when she finally opened her eyes, an unreadable expression on his face. Anger, somehow mixed with…want. Concern.

She explained about the man she'd seen when checking in last night and then how he'd pulled into the garage in his SUV and called out to her.

Christopher's jaw ticked. "Did you get his plates?"

"No."

"I'll get footage from the security staff at the hotel. Otherwise I'll look into whoever operates this garage. One way or another—I'm finding out who he was. Even if I have to hack into their damn systems myself. License plates, names, everything."

"It's probably nothing—just some creep chasing after women."

He raised an eyebrow.

"Some men are pigs," she said with a shrug.

"I don't like it," he said, his voice steel.

"Christopher—"

"I'm not letting anything happen to you. Not after finally finding you again."

The emotion in his voice startled her. He sure wasn't acting like someone who didn't give a damn. True, he had come back to her apartment, years ago—eventually. But her heart was already shattered by then. He wasn't the man she thought that he was. She couldn't be with a guy who ran every time he panicked. Not then; not ever. And the concern he was showing right now? It was too much. She didn't want any of the thoughts or memories currently racing through her mind. She wanted to forget about Christopher. The fact that he'd shown up in her life again all these years later meant nothing.

She pulled away and bent down to pick up her briefcase. She'd go back to her hotel room and pretend this little encounter never happened. Whatever the hell he wanted would just have to wait. She wouldn't get answers by ignoring him, but maybe the truth wasn't worth it anyway. Sometimes the past was just too damn painful to revisit.

"So that's it?" Christopher asked, crossing his arms in irritation.

"What's it?"

"I tell you I'm not letting anything happen to you, and you act like you're leaving." His thumb jerked toward the stairwell.

"I guess we're both good at that."

She turned, and his hands were on her in an instant. He pulled her close, his large body hovering behind her as an avalanche of shivers raced down her spine. He towered above her, his chin atop her head, and she crashed into his solid chest, loving a little too much the way her body fit perfectly against his. She felt safe. Shielded. His warmth and scent surrounded her. His lips brushed against her hair. She was drowning in him.

His hands flexed, digging into her waist, sending her mind reeling. One move, and he could turn her around and pin her against the wall, kissing her senseless. Proving her wrong. All his power and strength was attractive. Arousing. His entire body was tense, ready to spring at any moment, and she felt his thick arousal against her lower back. Liquid heat began to pool at her center.

"Why the hell are you here anyway?" she asked, her voice shaking. "Last I checked, Navy SEALs don't live in oceanfront hotels."

"I came here for you," he growled.

She pulled away and spun around to glare at him. Heat flushed her cheeks. She was aroused, angry, and everything else in between. How dare he chase after her now. He had his chance ten freaking years ago, and he blew it. "You shouldn't have come. Actually, no, you never should have left in the first place. But that's on you."

His eyes narrowed, and he stepped closer, forcing her to tilt her head back to meet his gaze. No way was she letting his size and strength intimidate her. Christopher was angry. Turned on. Her mouth dropped open in surprise at the heat in his eyes. Ten seconds ago he was ready to pummel whoever had been in the SUV. He'd been worried about her. Now he looked only like he wanted to haul her over his shoulder and not let her out of her hotel room until morning. To work out whatever it was still brewing between them between the sheets. Repeatedly.

"Walking out on you was the biggest fucking mistake of my life. I've regretted it every single day since. I'm not sure how the hell I got lucky enough for you to show up in my life not once but twice, but I know there's still something here between us. Last night was pretty damn amazing, and as long as you're here, I can't keep my hands off you."

His eyes softened as her lower lip began to tremble. She couldn't keep doing this dance with him—not tonight, not ever. Maybe he did regret the past, but that didn't mean their future was any different. Life would go on as it had—without

Christopher.

"Come with me tonight, Lexi."

"I'm not going anywhere with you. Last night shouldn't have happened."

He flinched, and his lips pressed together. "Not to your hotel room. Let's take a drive, me and you. We'll go to the beach just like old times."

She searched his brown gaze, trying to summon the strength to tell him no. There were a thousand reasons that she shouldn't go anywhere with this man, but a tiny part of her yearned for what once was. For the girl she'd once been.

"I need to change."

"I'll wait."

"Meet me back here in twenty minutes."

"Some guy spooks you in the garage, and you think I'll let you meet me right here? Not a chance in hell."

Lexi rolled her eyes.

"I'll pick you up in front of your hotel. Twenty minutes, or I'm coming up after you. And no one will be able to keep me from tearing the goddamn door down."

Chapter 10

Christopher pulled to a stop at the secluded north end of Virginia Beach, Lexi tucked safely into the passenger seat of his truck. It was quiet here, peaceful in the waning evening light. The lazy red sun was dropping in the sky behind them, seagulls swooped down through the air, and powerful waves crashed against the sandy shore. It reminded him of nights with Lexi a lifetime ago—of beers and bonfires on the beach when they'd both been young, foolish, and carefree. When he'd been high on life and love and hardly a damn thing could bring him down. When he'd make love to his girl until morning.

Seeing the pain on her face when she'd shot him down the morning after their fight all those years ago had crippled him. She'd been the one good thing in his life, and he'd thrown her away, like garbage. When her roommate had shown up a week later, telling him Lexi was long gone, he'd felt like his goddamn heart had been ripped from his chest. The hole had been vacant for years, empty and aching, and until he'd seen Lexi the other night at Anchors, he hadn't quite realized she held the missing piece.

Nearly ten years had hardened him—he'd seen more damage and destruction as a SEAL than he could've ever imagined. He'd been so hurt by Lexi's inability to forgive him that he hadn't ever been in a serious relationship since. That and the fact that she was the one his body craved. Fighting with his men for those who needed help made him prouder than damn near anything. But doing right by his girl? He'd be on top of the world.

Lexi glanced at him from the passenger seat, looking hesitant, wary. She'd been angry last night, furious this morning, but at the moment? She mostly looked defeated. The sadness filling her violet eyes was overwhelming. He'd give her anything she wanted just to have her stop looking at him that way.

Long black hair cascaded down to the floral sundress she wore, trailing across her bare shoulders and collarbone. Her cheeks were slightly flushed. She was so feminine and beautiful it ached just to look at her.

Reaching across the seat, he took her delicate hand in his. His thumb lightly caressed her knuckles, and she closed her eyes. He'd do anything to know what was on her mind—to take any sadness she had away.

"Let's go for a walk," he said huskily.

She looked out the window, refusing to meet his gaze. "I think I should go back to my hotel. This wasn't a good idea."

"Just hear me out," he insisted. "If you still want to leave after that, I'll drive you back."

And beg you to give me a second chance.

She sighed and agreed, pulling her hand away. She was out the door before he could assist her, and he grumbled as he jogged around the truck and again took her hand. Her sundress blew in the breeze, dancing around her shapely legs. She'd kicked off her sandals and stood barefoot, looking innocent and unsure. He laced his fingers between hers and tugged her down toward the water so they could walk alone along the deserted beach. The wind blew in off the ocean, and Lexi shivered. Late summer days gave way to cool evenings, and Christopher was more than happy to tuck her under his arm.

Right where she belonged.

"Why'd you leave Coronado?" she asked, surprising him. He expected about a million different questions from her, but that one wasn't even on the list. She knew his mom was there in California, and he'd planned to stick around to help her out. As much as he could anyway, since his SEAL team deployed frequently. He sent his mom money every single month, thinking she deserved a break after struggling to support him for so many years. Hell, his own goddamn father had failed to provide for them in any way.

"It was too hard to stay," he admitted. "Every single thing there reminded me of you. The beach, my apartment, even the damn FA-18 Hornets racing across the sky."

"You remember watching them together on the beach."

"You were the best thing in my life, Lexi. After you left, I couldn't even walk around base without imaging you there. I was a complete and total mess."

She looked up at him in surprise, shock crossing her face. He stopped and turned Lexi to face him, resting his forearms on her slender shoulders. She gazed up at him, leaning her head against his arms like a pillow. His gut clenched at how right it felt to hold her close. She was fragile and feminine. Sweet and caring. He'd fucking hurt her because he couldn't get his shit together back then. Because he hadn't dealt with his past.

He'd grown as a man in the years they'd spent apart, and he'd never let any harm come to her again. From him or any other man. The thought of her with another, however, made his blood boil. After having her last night, he couldn't fathom letting another man snatch her away. Not when they'd finally found one another again.

"Lexi, I never should have walked out that night," he said, his voice thick with emotion. "It was wrong for a thousand different reasons—the crux of which was hurting you."

"You were an asshole," she whispered.

"I was a scared kid," he said, stepping even closer. "My own dad walked out on me—just vanished. It was for the best, as messed up as that sounds. He used to hit me and my mom. I tried to defend her, but I was just a kid. He drank, and then he beat us."

Lexi looked up at him in horror, tears brimming in her eyes. "Why didn't you tell me? I would've helped you." A lone tear slipped down her cheek, and he tenderly wiped it away before clasping his hands behind her again.

"I never wanted kids because I was afraid I'd do the same damn thing. I was worried that any child of mine would be better off without me."

"You'd never do that!" she insisted, looking angry. "How could you even think that?"

He nodded grimly, words escaping him. Lexi believed in him, was his staunchest supporter, and he'd ruined everything.

"But why the hell would you ask if the baby was yours? You knew, you knew, I'd never been with another man. You hurt me."

Christopher clenched his jaw, his eyes filled with regret. "I'm sorry. If I could take it back—take everything back—I would. I asked myself a thousand times why I didn't chase after you, why I said that. I was scared out of my mind and a complete fool. I don't deserve your forgiveness, but my God, Lexi, I'd do anything for a second chance."

She wordlessly watched him, and the pain in his chest nearly was unbearable. "Lexi, I was so panicked that night I couldn't see straight. I bolted, tried to run from my fears. If I could do it over, I would. In a heartbeat. I drove around aimlessly for hours thinking, just needing to be alone, and then I watched the sunrise. I came back the second I realized—" he broke off, clenching his jaw.

"Realized what?"

"That I was in love with you."

Tears spilled down her cheeks.

"Please don't cry; I can take bad guys shooting at me, broken bones, bruised body parts…but I swear to God, Lexi, I can't take your tears."

***

"You should go," she said, hastily swiping them away as she tried to pull away from him. Stupid emotions. She was the picture of professionalism at work, but get her around Christopher, and she was an emotional wreck. She'd bottled up her emotions for years, and a few minutes with the man and she was crying and coming and feeling more than she'd felt in a decade.

He didn't move a muscle.

"You should go," she repeated.

"Honey, the US Navy couldn't drag me away from you."

His lips brushed against the top of her head. It was soft, sweet. Completely at odds with his usual alpha male, dominating ways. She looked up at him in confusion, and his thumbs wiped away the tears beneath her eyes. He ducked his head lower and kissed her softly. Heat burst through her as his mouth moved over hers. He took his time, slowly letting it build between them, as her body pulsed with awareness.

He pulled his arms from her shoulders and slid them down her sides, his fingertips skimming against the sides of her breasts, before he gripped her waist and hauled her into his arms.

She clung to him, desperately, legs and arms wrapped around this solid man. The sun had long ago sunk beneath the horizon, and a million stars dotted the night sky. You couldn't get this view down at the busy stretch of beach, but to the north, after the boardwalk ended and there was only ocean and sand, it felt like you could see the whole universe.

Christopher carried her to the bed of his truck, parked at the edge of sand near some dunes, and she realized he'd lay blankets there earlier. The hatch was already pulled down, and gently, he laid her on the soft cotton. The night surrounded her, the dark sky twinkling above. She shivered, and then Christopher's hands were on her, fisting her dress as he pushed it up above her hips. The night air kissed her bare stomach, and she trembled.

His lips dragged across her flat stomach. Hot. Hungry. She gasped at his warm mouth on her chilled skin, unwittingly arching up beneath him. His tongue swirled around her belly button, teasing. He kissed his way to her hipbone, his teeth grazing her. Marking her. Tonight she was completely his. She'd go back to the Pentagon, eventually. She had her career with the DoD, and Christopher had his in the Navy. But tonight, she needed to be that young girl again, completely smitten with her handsome Navy SEAL.

He ducked his head lower, his nose skimming across her panties as he inhaled her arousal. "So fucking sweet," he muttered. He kissed her through the lace, leaving her hot and aching. She was swollen and wet—for him. Desperate for his touch. No other man had ever pleasured her this way—although she'd slept with several in the years since leaving California, she'd never let a man kiss her so intimately. Only him.

His fingers slid in the waistband of her panties, gently pulling them down her legs. Rough hands spread her thighs apart, opening her to his gaze. Baring her completely to him. She trembled as she watched his eyes darken in the moonlight. He kissed his way up the soft skin of her inner thigh, taking his time, leaving her gasping. The whiskers of his five o'clock shadow scraped across her tender flesh. He skimmed his nose across her mound, not stopping, kissing and nipping at the skin on her other thigh.

His face hovering so close to where she needed

him was making her crazy. Frantic. She cried out and arched up, desperate for his touch. His fingertips skimmed up her seam and then teased her soft folds, already dripping with slick arousal. He caught her gaze for a moment as he touched her, letting his fingertips caress her. Christopher dipped one finger into her center, swirling arousal around her throbbing bud. Waves of desire enveloped her, each touch guiding her higher, closer to the precipice. He stroked her softly as her eyelids slid shut, the pleasure exquisite. The little whimpers and mewls coming from her mouth were sounds she'd never heard before.

"Do you like that, honey?"

Heat swirled through her, coating her skin with warmth. She felt drunk in her desire for him, dizzy and lost to everything but his expert touch. He removed his fingers, and before she could protest the loss of his touch, his mouth was upon her. Kissing, sucking, drinking in her sweet ambrosia. His tongue laved against her folds, delving into her swollen flesh with the fervor of a man starved. His tongue probed her wet center, nearly shattering her right then and there. Gentle thrusts in and out had her squirming, bucking against his mouth.

His tongue slowly trailed up, stroking softly against her clit. She gasped at the sweet pleasure as heat coiled down from her center, spiraling out through her body until every single nerve ending was alight from his touch. Thick fingers penetrated her, filling and stretching her silken walls. She moaned from the wonderful pressure. He crooked his fingers, touching her sensitive flesh deep inside, and sucked her clit into his mouth. Waves overtook her, buoying her up, pulling her under.

Hands and mouth sped up their movements, driving her wild, and she exploded. Her body bucked helplessly as she screamed into the night, the powerful onslaught nearly too much to bear. Her sex fluttered against his mouth and tongue; her inner walls clenched tightly around his thick fingers. It was too much, not enough, and her climax went on and on as Christopher never let up, determined to wring every last ounce of pleasure from her.

At last she lay there, gasping for breath, and Christopher hauled himself over her small frame. Undoing his trousers, his thick erection sprang out. Even in the moonlight, she could see the engorged head, dripping with his arousal, ready to sink into her soft folds. He rubbed himself against her slickened sex and then lined himself up, slowly penetrating her as she moaned, her walls still pulsing around him. He sank in balls deep and held still, pinning her to the bed of his pick-up, holding her right where she belonged.

Christopher slowly pulled out and sank back into her softness, making love to her gently, sweetly. He kissed her, murmuring sweet words in her ear neither of them would likely remember in the morning, they were both so far gone in pleasure and lost in one another. His thick length stroked her, claimed her as his, filled her in a way no other man ever could. His thrusts grew faster, harder, building her up once more as she panted for breath. Her orgasm exploded from nowhere, Lexi crying out again his solid frame, bucking beneath him. Christopher immediately followed, hardening even more before releasing his seed deep inside her.

His hands slid beneath her head, cradling it, and he kissed her. It was tender, sweet, the kiss of a man who'd gone years without making love to a woman. Maybe he'd slept with other women during their time apart, but this moment, this night? He'd made love to her. Passionately. Thoroughly. With his cock buried deep inside her, his hard body covering hers, and his lips on her mouth, she was lost only to him.

Deep brown eyes met hers, he kissed her once more. Completely. Possessively. Making her feel like she was the only woman in the whole wide world.

Chapter 11

Christopher muttered a curse as he glanced, bleary-eyed, at the text on his phone the next morning. It was five freaking a.m., before the sun had even risen, and they wanted him back on base in thirty minutes? What the fuck was going on?

Lexi lay naked beside him, bathed in the earliest light of morning. She was securely nestled in his arms, and they both were buried beneath the plentiful blankets he'd piled in the back of his truck. It was cool, probably only in the fifties, but with the warm blankets and the heat they'd generated throughout the night as their bodies joined, they'd created enough heat and combustion to power a locomotive. For an entire year.

Her warm body tucked against his was the sweetest thing in the world. She curled up against him like she was his. Lexi was so small and soft compared to his mass and strength, and he'd held her close and kept her warm all night long. A soft sigh fell from her lips, and he brushed a kiss against her soft cheek, regretting that he had to wake her up so that he could get to base.

The buzzing of the phone in her purse jarred him back to reality.

What in the hell?

He nudged her awake, his breath catching as violet eyes met his.

So fucking gorgeous.

"What's wrong?" she asked, her voice heavy with sleep as she met his concerned gaze.

"I just got called back to base. And your phone's buzzing as well."

She abruptly sat up, blankets falling around her, and her full breasts caught his attention, all creamy skin against rosy nipples. She shivered in the cool morning air and quickly wrapped a blanket back around herself. This was not the fucking time to feast on Lexi again, but holy hell. The woman was a sight to behold. What he wouldn't give to wake up beside her each morning. He wanted Lexi in damn near every way a man wanted a woman. If that included making her his forever, then so be it. He'd loved and lost her once but didn't think he could survive losing her again.

Lexi flashed him a knowing smile as his eyes slid back up her body. She reached across the back of the truck for her handbag as his cock stood to attention. She looked like a goddamn seductress sent down from heaven only for him. Like a goddess bathing in the early morning light. He wanted to roar in approval at having taken her in his truck last night—at making her come again and again for him. The next time he had her, it would be in his bed. And hell if he'd ever let her leave without agreeing to be his forever.

She flicked her raven hair over her shoulder as she bent forward, her eyes narrowing as she looked at the screen.

"Damn it. I'm supposed to be there, too. Who the hell is Commander Ryan Mitchell?"

Christopher's gut churned. "My CO. Why the fuck is he contacting you and me at this hour?"

"Do you think it's about the hackings?"

"Don't know why else he'd contact you. He's the one who asked me to sit in on your briefing yesterday. But he's in charge of my SEAL team, not network security on base. This makes no sense." Christopher scrubbed a hand across his face. They'd gotten little sleep for the second night in a row, and he'd hoped to take Lexi back to her hotel for a hot shower for two and room service. Now they'd have to book it to get to base on time.

Lexi tossed her phone into her bag and rustled around in the blankets. She slipped on her bra, making his mouth water at the sight of her lace-covered breasts. Unaware of his reaction to her, she looked around. "Where's my dress?"

Christopher snatched her sexy black panties from beneath where he sat. "Are you gonna let me keep these?" he asked, his eyes glinting.

"Give me those," she chastised, reaching for them. Christopher hauled her into his arms and up over his shoulder as he hopped down from the bed of the truck. He was hard as steel; thank God no one was around to see them both frolicking here naked on the beach. He had a massive hard-on and a nearly naked woman slung over his shoulder. Hell if he didn't wish they could stay here forever—just the two of them, alone by the sand and water.

A breeze blew off the ocean, rustling the sea grass that grew up by the dunes. People would be along soon—early morning walkers, maybe even a few military guys getting in a long run before a day on base. But for the moment? The deserted beach was theirs.

"Put me down!" she shrieked. He lightly swatted her bare ass with his hand, loving the way she squirmed. He could have her wet, dripping for him in no time, and regret filled his chest at being unable to spend any time this morning kissing and loving on Lexi.

"I'm taking you to dinner this weekend."

"You want to talk about this now, while I'm half naked?"

"I want to do lots of things with you half naked— preferably fully naked." It was hardly a time to be fooling around, but hell if he didn't feel lighter than he had in years waking up with his woman at his side.

His woman.

He liked the sound of that too damn much.

His hand palmed her bottom, briefly skimming over the smooth skin. The round globes of her ass were driving him insane. Unable to stop himself, he turned his head and gently sank his teeth into one bare cheek, marking her, letting her know she was his. She shrieked and squirmed more, and he could smell the scent of her arousal.

"Fuck, baby. I'd give anything to stay here this morning with you." He gently set her down in the soft sand, handing her the panties he'd held tightly in his grip. She slipped them on, her violet eyes wide with arousal. He snagged her sundress from the back of his pick-up, not liking the sight of her shivering in the morning air. As she slipped on her dress, he tugged on his boxer briefs and pants, then grabbed a blanket, wrapping it around Lexi like he would a small child. His lips brushed against the top of her head, the sweet smell of lavender slamming into him.

"Tell me you'll stay here with me," he said, his voice thick.

"We have to get to base," she said uncertainly.

"Here down at Little Creek. I can't stand having you tucked away at the Pentagon, not after finally finding you again."

Her face fell. "Christopher, I've built my career there. I can't just up and leave."

He didn't like the uneasiness settling in his gut. If he hadn't been such an ass, they could still both be back in Coronado, living happily ever after and all that shit. He was the reason she'd fled across the country, had built a successful career for herself at the Pentagon, and was no longer within his reach. The ache in his heart was his fault alone. But he'd be damned if he'd let her go without putting up the fight of his life.

**

Lexi took another sip of her scorching black coffee as she strode down the hall beside Christopher. He'd dropped her back at the hotel, and she'd taken the fastest shower of her life before putting on a black suit and speeding over to base. Not without stopping for a little high-octane to fuel her morning. She'd woken sleepily in Christopher's arms, content and ready for a lazy morning of lovemaking before heading in, and instead she'd been yanked from her slumber, called in for what was likely another screw-up relating to the hackings.

Christopher had greeted her in the parking lot on base, guiding her through a labyrinth of corridors. Her heels clicked against the hard floors, and Christopher grumbled beside her. He was all business compared to the softness he'd shown this morning— jaw clenched, shoulders pulled back, face set in stone. She wasn't sure if he was angry they'd been called in so early or upset she'd said she'd eventually return to the Pentagon. There was no time to wonder now, because after turning the corner, they were standing in the office of his CO.

A tall, hard-looking man in his mid-forties stood before them. He had dark hair cropped short with traces of gray around the temples and stormy gray eyes. He was massive and intimidating. Despite being older than Christopher, he looked like he could hold his own against a younger man. An equally intimidating man around Christopher's age stood beside the commander, with dark hair and cool blue eyes.

"Sir," Christopher said, saluting the older man. "Patrick," he nodded at the other guy.

Commander Ryan Mitchell introduced himself to Lexi and asked them all to be seated. She sank down into a chair beside Christopher, crossing her legs. She was used to sitting in meetings with military officers at the Pentagon, but Patrick's cool blue gaze had her shifting uncomfortably in her seat. He looked like he could be a member of Christopher's SEAL team, he was so big and massive, but he wasn't one of the men she'd seen the other night at Anchors. His gaze swept between her and Christopher, a knowing look on his chiseled face.

Freaking fantastic.

"This is Patrick Foster, leader of SEAL Team Alpha," Ryan said. His gray gaze settled on Lexi.

Patrick caught her eye and nodded.

"What's this about?" Christopher asked, eyeing his commander.

Ryan cleared his threat, glancing between the two of them. "As you know, Lexi's been sent down from the Pentagon to address the attempted hackings."

"Yes, sir." His lips pressed tightly together, his face giving nothing away. This man was the hardened SEAL, the warrior. He was all business meeting with his CO and didn't even bother to glance in her direction.

Lexi nodded at the senior officer, her face flushing. Christopher seemed unaffected, unfazed. His face was set in hard lines. Maybe he was good at compartmentalizing his feelings, but he'd made love to her all night long. Kissed her intimately, thoroughly. It was difficult to pretend there was nothing between them. She could practically feel the heat radiating off his large frame.

Lexi cleared her throat. "Did something happen overnight pertaining to the attempted hackings that we're unaware of?"

"You met Captain Edwards, head of network security on base, yesterday."

She nodded in agreement.

"What did you think of him?" Patrick asked, cool blue eyes assessing.

Lexi looked back and forth between Patrick and

Ryan in confusion. "He was very persistent. He checked in with me several times throughout the afternoon, kept wanting to know the status of the progress we were making. He was just...."

"What?" Patrick asked

"I got a strange vibe from him."

"In what way?" Ryan asked.

Lexi shrugged. "Honestly, I didn't like the way he looked at me."

Christopher stiffened beside her. She had an urge to reach over and grab his hand, or run her hand down his arm in a soothing gesture, but that certainly wasn't appropriate at the moment.

"We've received some intel that he may be playing dirty," Ryan said, his gaze flicking back and forth between Lexi and Christopher.

"Sonofabith," Christopher muttered.

Lexi cocked her head to the side, her eyes narrowing. "He's the one attempting to hack into the systems?"

"He's involved," Patrick clarified.

"He set it all up," Lexi marveled. "All the attempted hacks were to cover his tracks—to keep us running on a wild goose chase."

"That's what we fear," Ryan said. "You'll continue working with the rest of the staff this week, as planned. But I want you and Christopher working on this after hours. That's why I asked him to sit in on the briefing yesterday. He's a computer expert, despite his role here as a SEAL. His involvement in the briefing yesterday wasn't questioned due to his skill set. But we don't know who else may be working with Edwards. We need this taken care of under the table. Find proof that Edwards is involved, and he'll be court-martialed. Find out who he's working with. Whoever is on the outside that wants this info will be taken care of. I don't have to remind either of you that this is top secret, sensitive military information. The repercussions of said data leaking out into the public would be astronomical."

A chill snaked down Lexi's spine. Working to uncover hackers located at the ends of the Earth was one thing. They were hidden behind computer screens, burying themselves in lines of code. She'd smoke them out but never actually come face-to-face with any of them. Working to uncover the betrayal of a US naval officer, on base, a man who held security clearances and credentials to do anything, was quite another. Edwards had already creeped her out yesterday. How was she supposed to act nonchalant around him all week? How could she look him in the eye knowing his end game?

"Why the hell would be betray his own country like that?" Christopher asked, clenching his fists. His entire body tensed, looking ready to pounce and unleash its anger.

"Money. Greed. Power. Take your pick," Ryan ground out.

"How'd you get pulled into his?" Christopher asked, his gaze sliding to Patrick. Lexi wondered the same thing. Certainly the SEALs had their own missions and training. Why any of them were involved defied explanation. Just because Christopher was a computer whiz who could hack into anything didn't mean there wasn't a guy already on the IT staff who could be trusted to assist with outing Edwards. Did they really trust know one?

"I've got a few friends at the Pentagon. I asked

around, and they recommended Lexi be the one to come down here."

"Hell," Christopher muttered.

Lexi's gaze flicked to Patrick. The man didn't even flinch under her questioning gaze.

"See what you can find out this morning," Ryan continued. "Edwards will be here by oh-eight-hundred, so you don't have much lead time."

"Roger that," Christopher said, standing.

Lexi stood beside him, tossing her empty coffee cup into the trash. "Let's go," Christopher said, finally addressing her for the first time since they'd walked into the room. After saying their goodbyes, she followed him into the hallway, practically running to keep up with his brisk pace.

"What's wrong?" she asked.

"We've got a traitor on base, and Patrick pulled you down here on purpose," he said, his voice cold.

"Yeah, I gathered that. So what the hell's your problem? This is my job."

Christopher abruptly halted, his hand lightly gripping her arm. His thumb skimmed across the sensitive flesh on the inside of her elbow, and she softened.

"I don't like him jeopardizing your safety."

Lexi laughed. "He didn't even know who I was. Chill out, sailor."

Christopher nailed her with a gaze. Warmth seeped through her at his touch, and the aggressiveness in his eyes rendered her speechless. Christopher was fiercely protective of those that he cared about, but the idea that he was angry with his SEAL team member for seeking her out was absurd.

"The only damn reason he did that was because of

me."

"That's crazy. I haven't even seen you for ten years. How the hell would he know who I was?" The answer registered the second it was out of her mouth. He'd told Patrick about her? Yes, she'd told her best friends about what an asshole her ex was, but what man talked about a woman he'd been with years earlier?

Only the kind that regretted what he'd done.

Shaking it off, she took a step away from Christopher. "Let's just get this taken care of."

"Lexi—"

She hurried down the hall. "It doesn't matter. We've got work to do. Let's put a keystroke trace on his workstation, maybe pull up the data of what files he's recently accessed. We need emails, phone records, and bank statements. If he's in on this with outsiders, he's getting paid. We nail him, and we've got the hackers. I'll be back in Arlington by the weekend."

She reached the door to the server room, but before she could punch in the keycode to enter, Christopher grabbed her waist with one large hand. She froze in front of him, the feeling of his massive chest against her back enticing. Unnerving. He stepped even closer, crowding her into the doorframe, and she could feel his erection through his trousers.

His hand brushed some of the hair back from her neck, holding it away in a firm grip, and his lips were hot on her flesh. She let out a soft moan and arched against him, unwittingly thrusting her breasts out. No doubt he had quite a view from behind her. The camisole she had on beneath her suit jacket dipped low. She hadn't expected any man to hold her this closely. She had work to do.

Christopher nipped at the tender flesh on her neck, and she gasped. His teeth grazed over her skin, sucking, marking her. Heat coiled down from her center, arousal dampening her panties.

"Someone will see us," she whispered breathlessly.

"Thank fuck no one's here yet," he growled. "Because right now you're all mine."

***

Christopher's breath caught as he pulled Lexi's curvy body against his. He could gaze down over her shoulder from this position at the full globes of her breasts. He longed to skim his fingers across the tops of them. To dip his tongue into that gorgeous cleavage. To kiss her swollen breasts and suck on her rosy nipples until she begged him for more.

"Let's go inside." His voice was dark. Desperate. If anything happened to Lexi, he couldn't stand it. He needed to have her again, to take her pleasure, and to give himself release. Blood rushed to his groin, making him uncomfortably hard. His balls tightened, on edge, ready to explode into Lexi's warm heat. His teeth grazed over her neck, commanding, domineering. She held still, and the little whimpers coming from her nearly made him come undone.

He hastily punched in the keycode, pushing her into the server room. A quick scan showed no one around. As the door clicked shut, he pushed her against it. It was cold in here, and her nipples pebbled against the silky top that she wore. There was no time for lazy lovemaking or restraint. He was taking her hard, making her his. Showing her what a fucking mistake it would be to ever leave.

He kissed the swells of her breasts, thanking the heavens above she had on another skimpy little top. He didn't have time to undress her. His thumbs grazed her nipples as he palmed her breasts, then his hands slid down, and he tugged up her skirt. It bunched around her curvy hips, leaving her skimpy little red panties on display for his viewing pleasure.

Holy shit. He was going to explode just looking at her.

He kissed her roughly, covering her sex with his hand, trying to restrain himself. She bucked her hips against him, and he slid his hand into her panties, tracing his fingers through her creamy folds. Her silkiness coated his fingertips, and he wasted no time rubbing her arousal around her throbbing center, leaving her panting for him.

"Come for me, Lexi," he commanded, circling his fingers faster and faster. She tensed, but he didn't let up. His fingers teased her, unrelenting, making her gasp, and finally she cried out. He covered her mouth with his, drowning out her cries of ecstasy. She trembled as he unzipped his trousers and pulled out his throbbing erection. He hitched one of her slender legs over his hip, pulled the red lace aside, and pushed his swollen head into her opening. She gasped and clenched down around him, her walls still pulsating.

She was so fucking tight, he tried to hold back, but his release was imminent. He thrust into her again and again, chasing down his own sweet surrender.

"Fucking hell," he muttered, ripping her panties right off. His hand slid under her other thigh, and he lifted Lexi up, pinning her against the door, holding her legs wide open. She was his for the taking.

Lexi bucked wildly against him, her sex clenching down around his throbbing shaft.

"Oh God, Christopher," she whimpered. Her face was flushed, her violet eyes wide, and her lips swollen and ripe from his kisses.

He slid a hand to where their sexes joined, rubbing his thumb over her swollen clit. She gasped and bit down where his neck met his shoulder, muffling what otherwise would have been a scream of pleasure. Her inner walls milked him, making him even harder, and he exploded, detonating inside his girl. Her limp frame collapsed against him, gasping for breath, and he softly kissed her forehead, which was damp with perspiration.

This crazed need to claim her was overwhelming. Unstoppable. He'd never get enough of Lexi in one week, let alone in a lifetime.

He met her gaze, her eyes a mixture of lust, desire, and sadness.

"Lexi, I—"

"Don't say it," she said, putting one finger to his lips.

He kissed her softly and then pulled himself from her velvety walls, feeling like a jackass for not having anything to clean her off with. He'd taken her against the door on base for God's sake. For some reason being around Lexi made him lose all control. He wanted to take her and claim her—to know she'd never be with another man again. At the moment, he'd give up damn near anything for her. His career, his life in the Navy. Whatever she wanted, she could have. If his being a SEAL was what would keep them apart in the future, then screw it. He'd get a job up in

Washington with the rest of the suits.

Lexi watched him, the expression on her face unreadable.

He slowly lowered her to the ground. Snatching her torn panties from the floor, he wiped her off before tugging her skirt back down into place. He stuffed the red lace into his pocket, and Lexi smirked.

He met her gaze. "No way in hell are the other guys looking at your sexy little panties."

"I can't say I was expecting you to rip them right off me."

"I have no control when it comes to you, honey."

"When this is over, I'm going back to Arlington. My life is there now."

The idea of losing her again was unfathomable. Not when he'd finally found what his heart had so desperately needed all these long years apart. "We'll see," he said, brushing a soft kiss against her forehead.

For the first time she looked uncertain, like maybe she didn't want this to end when the week was over either. He'd move heaven and Earth to make her his girl again. Just as soon as they nailed Edwards and stopped the damn hackers.

Chapter 12

Lexi tensed as Christopher leaned over where she sat. Hands splayed on the desk, muscular arms on either side of her body, caging her in—it was difficult to concentrate on anything but the man behind her. She quickly typed out the code needed to track the keystrokes on Edwards' computer. It'd be untraceable, but they'd have a clear view into all of his activities. Christopher made a sound in the back of his throat that sounded like a grunt of approval. Or maybe it was a groan of frustration, and he was just as aroused as she was, being locked together in close quarters like this.

After the frenzied, primal way he'd taken her against the door an hour ago, she'd barely been able to think straight. Her mind was swimming, overwhelmed by the power and control Christopher always had over her body. Holy crap. No wonder no ever man ever came close to making her feel the way she did when she was with him. He was large and in charge, and not at all hesitant to show her just how badly he wanted her. The attraction between them was powerful. Explosive. And once again becoming addictive.

Lexi had been trying to work quickly all morning, knowing the other men and IT staff would be here shortly. There was little time between when the night shift left and the daytime staff arrived for her and Christopher to have time alone in the server room. Christopher's CO had said he'd make sure no one entered, but she didn't want to worry about getting caught red-handed. They needed to get in and get out, maybe reconvene tomorrow morning to do a little more sleuthing. They had less than an hour left to collect as much data on Edwards as they could, and Lexi would work a lot faster if six feet of solid muscle hadn't been right behind her.

"I'm going to have to leave soon," Christopher said. "Everyone expects you to be working in here, but a SEAL would look suspicious since no one else is around."

"Maybe they'll think we're having wild, crazy sex in the server room," Lexi said with a smirk.

Christopher leaned even closer, his lips brushing against her ear. The hairs on her arms stood up, and she resisted the urge to shiver at his delicious closeness. "The only one who gets to think about you having sex is me. I'll fucking kill anyone who touches you."

"Chill out. Those guys are completely professional."

"And Edwards?" Christopher asked, rising to his full height.

She spun around in her chair and stood, having to tilt her chin up to meet his eyes. "I didn't like the guy, but he wasn't hitting on me, if that's what's got your panties in a twist."

His eyes darkened. "My panties in a twist? If I recall correctly, the only panties I have are yours. And I'm keeping them."

Heat rose within her, but she shrugged, not willing to let him have the upper hand. "I have plenty more. Keep them as a souvenir to remember me by."

"Fucking hell, Lexi. This isn't a game."

"No one said it was. But I've got work to do, and you're distracting me."

"I'm coming over to your hotel tonight."

The door to the server room opening had Lexi jumping back. Christopher turned, his large body blocking hers. She quickly turned and clicked on the mouse, closing out of what she was working on, pulling up the maps she'd plotted yesterday. She didn't have to see who was there to know that Edwards had walked in. Christopher's entire body tensed.

"I hope I'm not interrupting anything."

"Of course not," Christopher said smoothly as she stepped to his side. "Lexi and I go way back." There was a threat hidden beneath his words—don't mess with my girl. For once Lexi was glad Christopher could be so overprotective. Edwards had creeped her out yesterday, and knowing what she did now? It was hard to look him in the eye without spitting on him or letting him know what an asshole and traitor he was.

"I just stopped by to check on Lexi's progress," Edwards said, his eyes sliding to her. "Commander Mitchell mentioned you were in here. I didn't realize you knew so many of the SEAL team."

"I used to work in Coronado," she said. That only explained how she knew Christopher, but she wouldn't give him anything else. "I should get back to work."

"I'm on my way to grab breakfast. I'll check in with you and the IT staff later."

He turned and swiftly walked back out, leaving Lexi standing uneasily beside Christopher.

"I don't like this," he ground out.

"What's there to like?" she asked sarcastically.

"I'll come by after work."

"Yeah, we can compare notes. All the data I retrieved earlier is stored on a thumb drive. We can pull it up on my laptop and see if we can find anything solid."

Christopher's brown eyes bore into hers. "Be careful."

"Always am," she said.

He bent over and briefly brushed a kiss against her forehead. He looked like he wanted to say more but didn't. Instead he turned and walked over to the door. She watched him, waiting for him to turn around. He paused briefly at the door, his hand on the doorknob, his shoulders tense, but with a shake of his head he pushed it open and silently walked out.

***

"I don't fucking like this," Christopher growled later that morning, glancing around the locker room at the other members of his SEAL team. "There are too many loose ends, and Lexi's in there alone, flapping in the wind."

Every man was there, either sitting on one of the benches or standing, arms crossed, looking concerned. He and Patrick finished briefing them regarding the mole on base, and the anger that crossed their faces was mild compared to what would happen to Edwards if any one of them got their hands on him. It killed Christopher not to be able to go right up to that asshole and punch him in the face, knocking that smug look right off of it.

"We should take that bastard down," Brent said, punching a fist into his open palm. "If that data gets leaked, all of our info does, too. Names, addresses, ops, locations of bases around the globe. Fucking hell."

"We need solid proof," Christopher said. "We all know he's guilty. It doesn't do a damn bit of good without evidence."

"It has to be able to hold up in court," Matthew agreed, looking thoughtful. "They don't have enough yet to nail him?"

"What'd you and Lexi find out this morning?" Patrick asked, clenching his jaw. Steel blue eyes slid from Matthew to Christopher.

"We put keystroke software on his workstation. We'll know everything he does here on base. Lexi hacked into his bank records—he's been collecting payments from someone. Apparently that asshole wasn't smart enough to at least have it deposited into an offshore account. Lexi checked, and there's nothing."

Matthew chuffed out a laugh. "You two are meant for each other. Hacking into every damn thing."

Christopher nailed him with a gaze. "Try telling her that."

Brent grinned. "Is your lady not satisfied?"

"Fucking hell," Christopher spat out. Jesus, you couldn't have serious conversation with the guy. One second he was ready to take out Edwards single-handedly, and the next he had women on his brain again. And not just any woman—Lexi. He sure as shit didn't want Brent imagining Lexi being satisfied by anyone—even if he was the one doing it.

"So what do you need us to do?" Evan asked. Concerned filled his gaze.

"Keep an eye on Edwards. He walked in on Lexi and me this morning."

Brent chuffed out a laugh, and Christopher shot him a look that could kill. "There are other members of the IT staff working with Lexi, so it's unlikely she'll be alone with him, but I don't trust that bastard."

"Lexi said this morning he made her uneasy," Patrick noted.

"Exactly," Christopher agreed. "I don't trust him."

"Hell, no one does," Mike said. "He's trying to steal sensitive data and sell it to the highest bidder."

"That's the least of my worries. Lexi is my priority," Christopher ground out. His gut clenched at the idea of anything happening to her. He'd been on edge last night when she was spooked over some dude in the parking garage. Now he had real worries to attend to—namely in the form of a traitorous Navy Captain.

Brent raised his eyebrows.

"She'll be under our protection," Patrick assured him. "I assume you'll be with her off base?"

Christopher nodded as Brent chuckled. Man, if he didn't want to punch that guy in the face sometimes. Brent would have his back if he needed him and would be livid if a man ever laid a hand on a woman. His own sister had been killed by a jilted ex-boyfriend, and Brent didn't tolerate any form of violence against women. Hell, none of them did. That didn't mean Christopher felt like dealing with his jabs at the moment. Or ever.

"Then we'll keep eyes on her here," Patrick said. "Tell her to avoid being alone with him."

The other men nodded in agreement. Christopher's mind flashed back to his SEAL team protecting Patrick's girlfriend, Rebecca, all those months ago. Life was strange, because he never in a million years would've imagined needing to ask them for help in protecting his woman. And he sure as hell never imagined the woman he couldn't fathom life without would once again be Lexi.

Chapter 13

Christopher muttered in disbelief as he stalked up and down Lexi's hallway. Where the hell was she? He'd told her he'd be stopping by this evening. She wasn't in her room, her car wasn't in the garage, and she wasn't answering her cell phone. Shit. Was she pissed about this morning? He shouldn't have taken her against the door like some goddamn animal, but hell. He'd barely been able to control himself around her, and somehow their bickering turned him on even more. She'd been sweeter than sin ten years ago, but this slight edge she had now? It nearly made him come undone.

He punched the button for the elevator and rode back down to the lobby. His eyes narrowed briefly as he caught sight of a hotel security camera. If she didn't make an appearance in the next hour, he'd check with them about reviewing the security footage. He knew he was overreacting. She'd probably just stopped by somewhere after work for dinner or a beer. There was no need to go all alpha male on her—it was barely after seven o'clock. Still daylight out. That didn't stop the worry that was winding its way through him. Christopher and the rest of the guys on his team had been trained to trust their instincts. To go with their gut. He had an uneasy feeling that something was wrong, and he didn't like it.

He quickly texted out a message to Lexi asking if she was okay. Even if for some reason she didn't want to talk to him, certainly she'd reply to that, right? He scrubbed a hand over his face in frustration. Waiting around here was like watching a damn pot and waiting for it to boil. Each minute that ticked by felt like an hour. He needed to move, to do something. Hell, even if he want for a jog along the beach just to clear his head and deal with the adrenaline surging through him, it had to be better than waiting around.

He sat down on one of the sofas in the lobby, the scowl on his face keeping anyone from approaching. He was in his uniform, so no one had asked him to leave. Not that they could've made him short of taking him out in handcuffs.

Thirty minutes later, Lexi walked in, wearing tiny little shorts and a tank top that clung to her curves, long dark hair swinging back and forth in a ponytail. His heart caught in his chest as he saw her, relief washing over him. What the hell had gotten into him? He'd been convinced she'd been hurt or in some sort of trouble, and here she was just out enjoying the evening sun.

"Lexi," he said, running over to her.

"What's wrong?" she asked, pulling her ear buds out. She had a small mp3 player strapped to an armband and had obviously been out for a walk along the beach.

"I've been trying to get a hold of you."

"Why? Did something happen?"

"Nothing happened," he growled. "I was worried something happened to you."

"I'm fine," she said, puzzled.

His gaze swept over her, taking in the swell of her breasts, the curve of her hips, and the way her toned legs stretched on for miles in those shorter than hell shorts. Blood rushed to his groin. Fuck. Every other man saw her on the beach like this, too. Did she even realize the affect she had prancing around in that outfit?

Two young women walked into the lobby just then, wearing skimpy bikinis, towels carelessly strewn over their arms. Okay. So maybe Lexi wasn't the most scantily-clad woman on the beach. But hell. Just looking at her had him harder than steel.

"Let's go up to your room," he said, grabbing her hand.

"I need a shower," she said, trying to pull free from his grasp.

His eyes flared. He laced his fingers between hers, her hand so soft and delicate in his own large, calloused one. "I won't say no to that," he said huskily, bending down. They stepped into the elevator and found themselves all alone. He pulled her against him, his chest to her back. He nipped at her ear with his teeth, tugging her closer to him. Wrapping their linked arms around the front of her body, he held her to him, his erection pressing into her back.

"How many times do you think I can make you come tonight?" he growled.

"We have work to do," she said, somewhat breathlessly.

"We'll get to it. But not before I have you crying out my name."

They hurried down the hall to her hotel room, Lexi practically running alongside him to keep up with his long strides. The door clicked open, and Christopher tugged Lexi inside along with him, guiding her into the bathroom. He turned on the shower, the hot water quickly filling the bathroom with steam. A second later, his lips were hot on hers. She smelled of the ocean, and he trailed his tongue down her neck, licking the saltiness off her skin. Fumbling, he pulled her tank top up over her head. Jesus. She had a tiny little string bikini on beneath it. One tug of those flimsy little straps, and she'd be bare to him.

He was harder than hell just imagining it. He knelt down before her, tugging her shorts down her legs. She kicked off her shoes and stepped out of both them and her shorts. In a daze, he kissed her flat stomach. She trembled at his touch, and he was dying to kiss her everywhere. His large hands rested on her hips, and he gazed up at Lexi. Her violet eyes were on his, lost in wonderment. Everything about her surprised him—she was sassy one minute and sweet the next. And for the next twelve hours, he had her all to himself.

He stood, quickly removing his uniform. His erection sprang out, thick and hard. Lexi stepped closer and gripped him, making him groan. Her thumb swirled over the crown, rubbing his arousal all over the head of his penis. He stilled, holding his breath. Any more of her touch, and he'd detonate, before he'd even touched her. That's how wound up she had him.

The tiny little triangles covering her breasts had to go. Her nipples were peaked beneath the fabric, and he needed to palm her, to take her into his mouth. Reaching one hand in the running water to check the temperature, he stepped into the shower. "Take off your bikini," he commanded.

Lexi looked startled for a moment but did as he asked, her hands trembling as she reached up to untie the straps behind her neck. The wisps of fabric fell away, and she reached behind her back, untying the remaining strips of fabric. She was gorgeous—full, soft breasts with rosy, pert nipples. He was about ready to haul her into the shower himself if she didn't hurry. She slid her hands into the waist of her bikini bottoms and bent, pushing them down her legs. The sight of her breasts bouncing before him nearly made him come undone. She was a goddess.

Lexi stood and stepped into the shower. He didn't even give her a moment, just pushed her back against the cold tile wall. The spray of water cascaded down around them, wetting her hair, sending drops of water down her face. He kissed her, groaning. She was so fucking sweet. His hands palmed her breasts, squeezing and kneading them. His erection pushed against her stomach. He slid one hand down to her sex, sliding his fingers into her folds. She was already wet, her arousal coating his fingers.

"Are you ready, honey?"

"Yes," she gasped.

He lifted her up against the wall and slid into her searing flesh, impaling her in an instant. She gasped at his sudden invasion, and he held still for a moment, letting her adjust to his size. He throbbed within her, his balls tightening as he tried to hold back. Lexi whimpered and tried to move against him, and he grabbed her hips, lifting her up and down his shaft. He thrust into her, taking all control, forcing her to surrender to the onslaught of pleasure. Her sex tightened around him as she clung to his shoulders, the little cries of pleasure coming from her mouth driving him insane. He ground into her again, rubbing himself against her sweet little clit, and she screamed, helplessly crying out as she rode him.

When she'd come down from her explosion, he pulled out then turned her around. Her palms splayed against the wet tile, and he pulled her hips back, stepping closer to her again. His erection teased her wet folds as he hunched down around her, one arm across her stomach, the other across her chest as he kneaded one breast. He entered her again, her walls still pulsing around his shaft.

It was sexier than fuck taking Lexi this way, holding her to him as he thrust into her from behind. She felt so damn tight in the position, he could barely stand it. He pumped into her as she moaned, and a second later, he exploded, releasing deep inside her tight channel.

Christopher pulled out and turned a trembling Lexi around, holding her tight against his chest. "You amaze me," he murmured, stroking her hair with one hand. He grabbed the shampoo from the side of the shower and began washing her hair, massaging her scalp as Lexi whimpered against him. The lavender scent of her shampoo was already making him hard again—or maybe it was just the stunning woman in his arms. She was warm, wet, and slippery, trembling against him as he took care of her.

He shielded her eyes and maneuvered them both under the shower spray, letting the soapy suds wash down the drain. Grabbing her washcloth, he applied a little body wash, then gently began rubbing it over her skin.

First he cleaned her back, gazing in wonderment at how tiny and perfect she was. Slender shoulders, narrow shoulder blades, smooth curves. The curve of her ass had his cock standing at attention again, but he turned her around and washed her breasts, bending over to kiss and suck on each one in between washing. She mumbled incoherently, and he knelt down before her, hitching one of her legs over his broad shoulder.

"Christopher," she whispered.

"I'm right here, honey."

His lips were on her sweet folds, and he kissed her and drank in her ambrosia. She was wet and swollen for him, and he softly sucked her clit into his mouth. He lightly tongued her, his hands grasping her hips, holding her against him. She held her breath, on the tip of the precipice, then cried out, her sex fluttering against his mouth and tongue as she came again.

He removed her leg from his shoulder and continued washing her body, cleaning her between her legs and then working all the way down to her feet. He stood and quickly scrubbed himself off as well, not even caring that he'd smell like lavender. Like Lexi.

***

Lexi awoke with a start, trying to sit up in bed. A muscular arm was wrapped around her, holding her close, and before she could panic, Christopher's soothing voice was in her ear.

"Lexi, it's me. What's wrong?"

"I, I don't know," she said, struggling to sit up.

He released her and sat up beside her, looking concerned. Hot skin covered chiseled muscle, and she tried not to gape at awakening next to a shirtless Christopher. Hell, she'd been with him hundreds of times—but the way he looked at her now? All buff and macho and concerned? It made her heart skip a beat.

"Did you have a bad dream?"

"I guess. I thought someone was chasing me. They wouldn't let me go."

Warmth filled his gaze. "You're safe, honey. I'm right here, and you know I'd never let anything happen to you."

"I guess. It just felt so real."

Christopher's large hand stroked her hair, trying to calm her. His massive bicep bunched as he moved, and the heat she always felt when she was with him flushed over her skin. She looked back up at him, and he pulled her into his muscular chest. "You've had a busy few days—and I haven't exactly been letting you get a lot of sleep. I'll stay with you every night until this is over."

"And after? What happens then?"

She shouldn't be spending time with Christopher at all, because that would just make it that much harder to leave.

"I'll do whatever you want," he said softly.

She nuzzled closer against his warm chest, loving the feeling of him holding her safe and close. She didn't want to answer that, didn't want to think about anything other than tonight—than this moment.

"Let's go back to sleep."

He laid her down, pulling her back against his chest. One arm wrapped around her, beneath her breasts, as he held her close. He kissed the back of her head, and she relaxed against him, exhaustion taking over. She could feel his arousal against her back, but the pull of slumber was too strong. Another time they'd make love until dawn again. Right now, she just needed him to hold her.

Chapter 14

Lexi pulled into Kenley's condo complex in Virginia Beach the following evening. Another busy day on base had her no closer to discovering who was behind the attempted hacks or to gathering enough information to convict Edwards. They were close—really close. But she wanted the final nail in the coffin before she turned everything over to Commander Mitchell. Christopher's CO had seemed concerned earlier, worrying that Edwards might sense they were onto him, and Christopher had promised to come to her hotel that night. He'd probably be angry she wasn't there, since he said he'd check on her, but she needed some time and space to clear her head. Seeing him would only lead to another night of mind-blowing sex, and in her blissed-out state, she wouldn't be able to think clearly.

Maybe he did regret their past and want a shot with her in the future, but that sure the hell didn't mean it was going to happen. She'd finish this job and head back to the Pentagon. He'd move on with his life, deploying to God knows where half the time, and she'd move on with hers. But would it really be that simple?

She used the spare key Kenley had given her earlier that summer to enter the empty condo and then called her best friend.

"What's up, hun?" Kenley asked. Lexi could hear the television blaring the background along with the whirring of machines and wondered if Kenley was at the gym.

"I'm at your parents' condo."

"What happened to the hotel?"

"I'm avoiding someone," she said with a sigh. She dropped her purse and keys on the kitchen counter and then strode over to the sofa, collapsing. All she had were her own gym clothes, which were still in her bag in the car. At least they were clean. She hadn't chanced returning to the hotel since she knew Christopher would be lurking around there, ready to pounce and kiss her senseless.

Senseless really was the right term for it, because whenever she was around that man she couldn't even think straight. How he managed to make her so mad and simultaneously aroused was beyond belief. They needed to bottle that stuff up as an aphrodisiac and sell it to the highest bidder. That man could convince her to do damn near anything. She'd loved him when she was younger, but that love had been young and innocent. So far their time together this week had been passion-fueled, fast, and furious. Unstoppable. Put them together and you didn't have sparks, you had a damn explosion.

Making love on the beach had been sweet and sensual, but yesterday morning on base and last night in the shower? Holy hell. That man got her hotter than anything, and she didn't trust herself to be left alone with him. He'd actually ripped her panties right off. And damn if that didn't make her hotter than ever for him. No wonder no other man was able to live up to Christopher—he took control, knew exactly what he was doing, and didn't let up until she was sated. She'd fallen for the sexy Navy SEAL when she was younger, but this commanding alpha male thing he had going on now was sexier than hell.

The more time she spent with him, the more she realized how hard it would be to return to the Pentagon. Harder than leaving years ago when she was furious with him. Maybe she could forgive and forget the past, but could she forget this week? He'd try to convince her to do the long-distance thing, no doubt. That or move down here and right in with him. How ironic that she'd been half considering transferring to a military base on the water. Not that she'd mention that to him—he certainly didn't need more reasons to convince her to stay.

"Would this someone be a tall, handsome, SEAL by any chance?" Kenley teased, bringing her mind back to the present.

"Is there any other kind?" Lexi asked with a laugh.

"I'm going to have to get down there sooner rather than later."

"To keep me from making a terrible mistake?"

"Hell no. To meet some of his hot SEAL friends."

"They're all as hard-assed as him."

"And what do you know about their asses? Have you engaged in a little sex with the ex yet?"

"No comment," Lexi muttered dryly.

"You have!" Kenley squealed. "I was planning to come down this weekend. Maybe I should take a few days and get there sooner."

"I'll be working on base all day. But we can hang out in the evenings if you want. Did you talk to Cassidy?"

"Yeah, she can't come this weekend."

"That sucks."

"You still have me. I'll come down Friday. I can chill out on the beach while you work all day—just as long as you promise to drag some hunky SEALs out for drinks with us Friday night."

Lexi sighed. "We'll see. I've got a crazy number of fires to put out down here first."

"Is everything okay?" Kenley asked, concern tingeing her voice.

"Yeah, it's just a little more complicated than I originally planned."

"The guy or the job?"

"Both," Lexi admitted. "The job is more complicated than I ever anticipated, and the last man on Earth I expected to see here was Christopher. But I'm glad you can come down this weekend. I'm not so sure this will be wrapped up in one week like I originally thought, so it'll be nice to get in a little girl time at the beach."

"Think we can watch those hunky SEALs training?"

"You're relentless," Lexi laughed. "But I promise, whenever I see Christopher again, I'll be sure to ask him about his single friends."

"Perfect. Talk you later, hun."

"Bye."

Lexi hung up and glanced around her friend's condo. It was a little ridiculous to be fleeing here. She didn't have her suitcase, didn't have any food or toiletries. She blew out a sigh. Maybe she'd head back to her hotel after all. No doubt Christopher would be swinging by later on, either asking to talk or whisking her off her feet. Maybe both.

She'd tell him she needed some time to process everything. Certainly he could understand that. Just because they'd been together once long ago didn't mean it was the right move right now. And until this entire mess on base was settled, she didn't have the time or energy to devote to man troubles. He made her lose all sense of control when they were together, and she couldn't think clearly if she spent another night in his arms. Maybe he did want to protect her, but it's not like anything could happen while she was tucked away safely in her hotel.

Standing, she walked back to the kitchen and grabbed her purse. Maybe she could order room service back at the hotel and have an early night. Christopher had kept her up until dawn several nights in a row, and with a couple of early mornings at Little Creek, she was running on fumes. Looking around the condo, she realized she'd left her briefcase down in her SUV. This wasn't a high-crime area, but leaving her laptop and tablet unattended was a bad move. She was more exhausted than she realized.

Locking up, she walked back out into the parking lot to her vehicle. It stood alone where she'd parked only half an hour earlier, and immediately, she sensed something was wrong. Hurrying over, she saw glass shards from the passenger side window scattered all over the black asphalt, gleaming in the late afternoon sun.

What the hell?

The glass crunched under her heels as she hurried to the door. An uneasy feeling of dread washed over her, and she quickly glanced around, making sure whoever had committed the crime wasn't still around. Her heart quickly palpitating, she scanned the area, clutching her keys tightly in her hand. The metal bit into her skin, but she gripped them even more tightly. If someone was still here, she wasn't going down without a fight.

The parking lot was empty, the only sound coming from a few birds chirping in the trees and some traffic down the block. A light breeze blew, rustling the leaves. Goosebumps coated her skin, but she spun around in a complete circle, and there was nothing. No one.

Her stomach dropped as her gaze fell onto the empty passenger seat. Her briefcase was gone.

Damn it.

Should she call the police? Call Christopher? Uncertainly, she looked around again. She could check with the condo office to see if they had surveillance cameras in the lot. Or hack into the nearby traffic cams to see if they'd caught something. A vehicle speeding away would be suspicious, not to mention highly noticeable, but what if the person had been on foot? People were coming and going all the time since they were right near the beach. It might be difficult to pick one person out from a stream of many. They had to have broken in during the past thirty minutes.

She groaned. All of the info she and Christopher had pulled was stored on her thumb drive. She'd stupidly tucked it away into a zippered compartment in her briefcase, but if the wrong person got a hold of it, they'd have clear insight into all of the research she and Christopher had done on Edwards. Phone records, bank accounts, emails, everything was stored there.

Shit.

Hopefully the thief was just some jackass looking for money or electronics. If somehow Edwards or someone else on the IT staff had realized that she and Christopher had been snooping around where they didn't belong, that could be bad news for everyone. She'd made sure to thoroughly cover her tracks, but damn. She was so exhausted she'd carelessly left her bag in the car. What if she'd made some other careless mistake on base today?

Worry bloomed inside her chest as she realized the seriousness of the situation. The information they'd retrieved couldn't fall into the wrong hands. It would jeopardize the investigation, not to mention her and Christopher's safety. Her chest constricted at the thought of harm coming to him. He was a freaking Navy SEAL—certainly he could handle himself. Why hadn't she kept the thumb drive on her person? Hell, she could've put it in her purse or tucked the damn thing into her bra, just to make sure it never left her sight.

She closed her eyes briefly as she tried to gather her thoughts. She needed a game plan. First, she'd go back to the hotel. Hopefully the concierge could assist with finding someone to repair her window. She'd call Christopher from there, letting him know they needed to meet ASAP. Maybe they'd involve the police, but if Edwards was somehow behind it, they should notify someone on base instead. And she'd have to call Kenley back, telling her not to come. The situation seemed to be growing more dangerous by the hour, and she didn't need her friends dragged into this mess, too.

***

Christopher drove down Atlantic Avenue after work, heading to Lexi's hotel. She'd seemed skittish today, and he wasn't sure if she was worried about Edwards or worried about him. Hell. He didn't need to be pressuring her into deciding what to do when this whole incident wrapped up. She'd go back to the Pentagon like planned. He'd drive up to DC to see her some weekends. Give her time to figure out what she needed. And then convince her that he couldn't live another day without her in his life—forever.

Now if they could just get this shit with Edwards taken care of, he'd be breathing a hell of a lot easier. The guy seemed suspicious that Christopher had been nosing around the other day rightfully so, As a SEAL, he didn't really have a damn good reason to be hanging out in the server room with Lexi. He'd been called to sit in on the initial briefing, but otherwise? He had to lie low, even though he wanted eyes on the bastard every second.

His phone buzzed in his pocket, and he pulled it out, glancing down to see his commander's face flash across the screen.

Fucking perfect.

He'd just left base ten minutes ago. If they were calling him back in or sending the team out on an op, he was going to lose it.

"Walters."

"Something's happened to Lexi," his CO said.

Christopher nearly slammed on the brakes as his blood ran cold. He gripped the steering wheel, his knuckles turning white. "Is she okay? What happened?" So help him, if anyone so much as touched a hair on her head, they were a dead man.

"Her car was found abandoned in a garage on Atlantic Avenue. Door was wide open, engine still running, and Lexi and her belongings missing."

"God damn it!" he shouted. "Where the fuck do you think she is?"

"Don't know. The Virginia Beach PD contacted security at Little Creek. Apparently her temporary parking ID was hanging from the rearview mirror. They got word to me a few minutes ago, and I figured you'd want to be the first to know."

"Damn right," Christopher said, his voice cold.

"I'm calling the team in. The fact that Edwards was playing dirty and Lexi was involved in tracing the attempted hackings means we need to track that mother-fucker down. I'd bet my life he's somehow involved. Get your ass over here ASAP."

"Already on my way," Christopher said, pulling an illegal U-turn in the middle of the road. Cars honked around him, slamming on their brakes, and his tires squealed as he sped up. The engine of his truck roared as he floored it, speeding back to base. If the cops were around to see that, they'd have to chase him all the way there. No way in hell was he stopping. Not when his girl needed him.

His heart was beating so furiously, it felt like it might pound right out of his chest. "God damn it!" he shouted again, punching the dashboard. His instincts had told him something was wrong, that Lexi could be in danger, and that was the whole damn reason he'd planned to be at her hotel each night. Hell. He should've been looking out for her more. He should've hacked into the phone network and tracked her GPS, known where she was at every moment.

The second he arrived on base, he was pulling up her phone records, consequences be damned. He didn't care if he didn't have legal authority to hack into the databases, but he wasn't wasting another second knowing harm had potentially come to his girl.

And what about the guy at her hotel that had spooked her the other day? Did he have something to do with it, to? That seemed as far out there as any other reason at the moment, but what else did they have to go on? A strange man watching her at her hotel, a traitor on base, multiple attempted hackings. Could anything else go wrong?

He flew down the road, cruising into the tree-lined street leading to base. He better slow down or the guards would be shooting at him, assuming he was planning to crash through the security barriers. With the way he felt at the moment, he'd take on the whole damn Navy if it meant getting Lexi back to him sooner.

Chapter 15

Lexi glanced around the darkened room in a daze as she slowly came to. Her brain felt foggy, like she was trying to remember something but couldn't quite grasp what it was. Shadows danced across the window, and she couldn't tell if it was morning or evening. She was cold. Uncomfortable. Her mouth was so dry it felt like it was stuffed with cotton. Her muscles were stiff and sore from the position she'd been sleeping in on the hard floor. She'd been tired earlier, but what the hell had happened after she left Kenley's condo? Where was she?

The room was empty save for the thin blanket and lumpy pillow on the ground. She cringed as she sat up, wondering the last time either of them had been washed. Bare cinderblock walls surrounded her, cold and sterile. The concrete floor was equally unwelcoming. Her hands clutched the dingy blanket beneath her as she tried to get her bearings. She still had on her suit from yesterday—or was it today? What time had she left Kenley's condo?

She leaned back against the cold wall, her head pounding. She had to think clearly—panicking in this situation wouldn't do her any good. Had someone taken her here? Was she hurt? She had to try to remember something, to fill in the gaps from leaving the condo and waking up here.

Glass shards had been all over the ground. Her window, her laptop….

She heard voices down the hall, arguing, and her chest clenched in fear. Were these the men that had taken her? Bile rose in the back of her throat as the sound began getting louder, the men getting closer. What did they want with her?

Her heart began to pound as the footsteps approached the room she was in. She felt nauseated and dizzy. She desperately wanted lie back down as the room began to spin, and she forced herself to take a deep breath, drawing in precious oxygen. She was tired. Disoriented. She needed to stay alert.

The footsteps stopped at the door. A key turned the lock.

She wrapped her arms tightly around her chest as the door opened. A man's designer shoe stepped in, and she looked up, taking in the man in the slick suit from her hotel. Another expensively tailored suit hung from his tall frame now. He was almost the height of Christopher, but not nearly as broad or strong. Not a piece of slicked back hair was out of place, and without his sunglasses, she could look right into his black, beady eyes. The overpowering, potent scent of his cologne permeated the room. She resisted the urge to vomit.

Hell.

He smirked as he watched her, a smile playing about his lips. "I don't think we've properly met," he said in a thick foreign accent.

"Where the hell am I?"

"Feisty, I like that. I can tell you're going to be a lot of fun."

She hugged herself more tightly so he wouldn't see her tremble. This guy wasn't so big—she could get in a few good jabs. Too bad her head was so foggy. Given the chance, she'd rip his balls right off if he tried anything. But certainly he wasn't here all alone. She'd heard voices in the hall a moment ago. Even if she did somehow manage to harm him, then who would come for her? And which was worse, the enemy you knew or the one you didn't…?

"Why am I here?" she asked, struggling to stand. Her legs felt like jelly. She couldn't run from him if she wanted to.

He appraised her, beady eyes scanning over her body. The hunger in them scared her more than her confinement in this room. This man had watched her at her hotel. Followed her. Found her. The last thing she remembered was driving back after leaving Kenley's condo. She'd made it to the parking garage, hadn't she? It felt like something was missing, like she couldn't recall what had happened next….

"You have information I need."

"I'm not telling you anything!"

He took a step closer, and she leaned back. Sitting on the ground, leaning against the hard wall, she had nowhere to go. She needed to stand up—to fight him off if necessary. Clumsily, she struggled to get to her feet. Her hands sought purchase on the wall, and as he watched her, she finally made it to a standing position. She leaned back against the cool wall to keep from swaying.

"You and your friend have been investigating someone on base. I need that information."

"Like hell you do."

"I think you'll cooperate when you see what I have to show you."

"Fuck you," she said, struggling to fight through the haze in her brain.

"Ah, I think my men may have given you too much."

Her mind swam. She'd been drugged. No wonder she couldn't remember a damn thing. What day was it? Christopher was supposed to meet her at the hotel. He'd realize she was missing. But was it night yet? Or had she been out of it for several days?

She had no sense of time—she could've been in this room for hours or a week. The man reached into his suit jacket, and she stiffened. She was almost relieved to see him pulling out photographs.

He took a step toward her, and she darted to the side, stumbling.

"I won't hurt you," he said in a thick accent.

She looked at him warily—no, he'd just drug, kidnap, and hold her against her will. Not to mention demand sensitive, military information.

He laughed, a loud, harsh sound. "Oh, I'll fuck you. Don't get me wrong about that. Women like you need to be flat on your back—maybe down on your knees, getting me off. You sure seemed to enjoy it with that Navy SEAL of yours."

She stiffened.

He tossed the photographs carelessly onto the

ground. "Take a look. You give me the information I need, and I won't release these to the public. But I will be back later—and whether you cooperate on this or not, you'll be mine tonight."

Her heart pounded in her chest, adrenaline racing through her system. What a sick, twisted bastard. Like hell she'd give him anything. And no way was he laying a hand on her. She'd rip his heart right out if he got a step closer.

He turned and walked back to the heavy door, yanking it open. With a quick glance over his shoulder, he leered at her again. "I especially like the first one, with his mouth between your legs. Stupid bitch."

The door shut behind him with a loud thud, and she heard the click of the lock turning. She scrambled down to the floor, crawling over on her hands and knees, scooping up the photographs. Certainly he couldn't—

Her heart stopped as she gazed at the pictures. Someone had photographed her and Christopher the other night on the beach. She was naked, in the bed of his pick-up, and Christopher was pleasuring her as she screamed in ecstasy. There were nude photos of her—of him. Of the two of them passionately making love. Her stomach churned, and she leaned over, spewing vomit all over the pictures.

***

Christopher ground his teeth as he eyed the other men on his SEAL team. Every man looked livid, but not a single one of them knew how he felt. When Patrick's girlfriend Rebecca had been chased by a stalker, she'd never been in imminent danger. They'd kept eyes on her at all times, and the stalker had ended up at Patrick's home. Evan's girl, Alison, had suffered a serious asthma attack and been hospitalized right before they were sent out on a mission, but again, they knew exactly where she as at all times. And she was alive. Breathing.

But not knowing what the hell had happened to Lexi? It was fucking killing him.

The police had discovered Lexi's purse on the side of the road not far from the garage, cell phone in it. There was no hope of tracking her that way, and Christopher's gut churned at the thought of someone taking her. It wasn't a robbery—they'd left her vehicle and ditched her purse. The only signs of a struggle were a broken window on the passenger side.

This was all his damn fault. He never should have let her out of his sight for a moment.

"The MPs have been sent to arrest Edwards," his CO informed the team. "Virginia Beach PD is looking at the security footage at the hotel's garage. A large black SUV was seen leaving around the time Lexi's car was discovered, but the plates were missing."

"Shit," Christopher said under his breath.

His CO's eyes swept to him.

"Lexi saw some guys in an SUV watching her the other day," Christopher explained. "She was freaked out at first but convinced me it was nothing. If I hadn't been there, they probably would've nabbed her then."

"What day was that?" Patrick asked, his eyes narrowing.

"Ugh, a day or two ago. Fuck, I can't think

straight."

"I'll call my buddy at the precinct. They can pull up the footage from a few days ago if you can give us an estimate of date and time."

Christopher took a deep breath, trying to steady his thoughts.

"I called a few people up at the Pentagon," his CO said. "They called Lexi's emergency contact—some friend of hers in Arlington. Apparently the friend has a condo down here, and Lexi was there earlier today."

"Let's search it," Mike said.

"Absolutely," Christopher agreed. "Did you get the address?"

"You and Mike head there," his CO commanded, spouting off orders. "Brent and Evan will head to the hotel to work with the police. Patrick and Matthew are here with me."

"We'll find her," Patrick said, cool blue eyes meeting his.

Christopher gave him a gruff nod, then took the address from his CO. He'd tear his hair out sitting around here doing nothing. Going to her friend's condo, knowing Lexi had been there hours before, gave him something to focus on. Some hope of finding a clue, tracking her down. His gut churned. He'd been sent out on missions all over the world, jumped out of airplanes, swam in dark, choppy waters. But nothing scared him as much as the thought of harm coming to Lexi.

Thirty minutes later, they were pulling into the parking lot at the condominium complex. Cars were parked throughout, but a man in khakis and a polo shirt stood at an empty space. He had a dustpan and broom in his hand, and Christopher noticed glass scattered on the ground.

"Don't touch that!" he shouted.

The man looked up, startled, to see two Navy SEALs heading toward him.

"This may be a crime scene," Mike said, grabbing the broom. "A woman who was here earlier is missing, and the window in her SUV was broken. Call the police and don't touch a thing."

"It's unusual to have crime in this area," the man said.

"My girlfriend was kidnapped," Christopher ground out. "She was visiting a friend here earlier this evening, and then her car was found abandoned in a garage. The window was smashed out."

"And you think this is it?"

"The police will confirm," Mike said.

The man agreed to place the call, and Christopher and Mike hurried to the condo. Glancing at the unit number, he was surprised to find the door ajar. Gesturing to Mike, the two of them silently entered. Their SEAL team was used to running ops together, busting down doors and searching the premises. Taking prisoners when needed. They communicated wordlessly, worked as one unit.

The team was more than well acquainted with searching hell holes in the Middle East, not luxury condominiums in beach towns near base.

Fucking hell.

There was a rustling sound coming from a room in the back, followed by the sound of drawers opening and closing, and the two men crept quietly down the hall. Maybe Lexi had left the door open and a robber had entered. Maybe one of her kidnappers had come back here looking for something.

A quick scan upon entering had shown the family room and kitchen to be empty, so whoever had entered was somewhere back here. Christopher pulled out his sidearm, following behind Mike. A shadow emerged from the doorway on Mike's left, and Mike was on the suspect in an instant, pinning them against a wall with his hulking frame.

The woman screamed hysterically, and Mike's large hand covered her mouth as he eased up.

"Who are you?" Christopher asked, eyes assessing. The woman looked positively terrified to see them. She was petite and small, with wavy brown hair and wide eyes filled with fear. She trembled as Mike's large frame held her in place. "Get the fuck off of her," Christopher barked.

Mike released her, grumbling a gruff apology.

The woman looked back and forth between them like she'd seen a ghost. Christopher didn't miss they way she remained back against the wall, scared out of her mind. "Do you guys know Lexi?"

"Yes, and she's missing," Christopher said, in as calm of a voice as he could muster. "Is this your condo?"

"It's my parents' condo. Someone at the Pentagon called me earlier," she said shakily. "I'm Lexi's emergency contact, and—" Her voice broke, and he could see the tears that threatened to fall.

Christopher reached out and roughly pushed Mike further away from the scared woman. He was hovering over her like she belonged to him or something, concern and unconcealed interest flickering in his blue eyes. What the fuck that was about, he didn't even want to venture. This sure as shit wasn't the time or place. "You're safe with us,"

Christopher assured her. "Lexi's been kidnapped, and we thought you were involved. The door to the condo is open."

"Oh, I forgot to close it," she said distractedly. "I just came in to look around. Lexi called me from here earlier. After someone from the Pentagon called and told me she was missing, I drove down as fast as I could."

"What time did she call?" Christopher asked, his eyes narrowing. Hell, this woman was another clue in the trail of where Lexi had been all evening, and Mike had practically frightened her to death. The woman hastily explained her phone call with Lexi earlier.

"I'm sorry, I didn't even introduce myself. I'm Christopher; this is my teammate, Mike."

"You're him," she finally said, eyes flicking up and down his frame.

"Him?" Christopher questioned.

"Her guy. The SEAL from Coronado."

"She told you about me?" He didn't know what to make of that. Had Lexi told her she'd run into him again this week? Or had she told her him in the context of her asshole of an ex-boyfriend? He had little to say to this woman in defense of how he'd acted all those years ago. But he'd fucking make up for it now. He wouldn't rest until Lexi was back in his arms. And if any harm came to her, he'd dig the graves of her kidnappers himself.

"Only a million times."

Christopher's chest filled with warmth, immediately followed by pain. Hell, his heart actually hurt thinking about her. Lexi certainly wouldn't have talked about him that much if she didn't still feel something over all their years apart. Maybe a reference or two in passing, but if Lexi's friends knew about him, a man from her past, apparently he wasn't out of her mind as much as Lexi had led him to believe.

"I'm Kenley," she finally said, holding out a small hand. He shook it, squeezing gently as if to reassure her. Or maybe it was himself he was trying to reassure. She glanced at Mike warily but didn't offer a handshake to him. Fucking idiot—pinning a defenseless woman against the wall. He was easily twice her size. He could have restrained her without going ape shit.

Christopher filled her in on the broken glass found in the parking lot. They looked around the condo but didn't see anything else amiss. If Lexi had been here, it hadn't been for long. But why had she come?

"Are you planning to stay here?" Christopher asked. "How can we get a hold of you?"

Kenley said she'd stay until Lexi was found, offering to help in any way that she could. They exchanged contact information, with Christopher promising to call as soon as they knew anything.

"I don't think that's a good idea," Mike said, his voice low.

"What's not?" Christopher asked.

"Her staying here alone."

Kenly glared at him, placing her hands on her hips. "I'm pretty certain the only person I have to worry about here is you."

Mike stiffened, and Christopher tugged him to the door. Jesus. They had to get a move on, and he sure as hell wasn't going to stand around keeping these two from tearing each other's throats out. He needed to call his CO, see if the police had any leads on the

SUV in the garage. If they didn't have anything by now, he'd hack into the damn traffic cams himself. Lexi was out there, alone. And nothing was going to stop him from finding her. This ended tonight.

Chapter 16

Lexi pinched the bridge of her nose, a headache forming. The combination of whatever they'd drugged her with, the lack of food and water, and the deep sleep she'd been in earlier was wearing her down. How many hours had passed since she'd been kidnapped? She wasn't even sure what day it was. Her stomach rumbled, but she felt too queasy to eat. Not that they'd offered her anything.

The sun dipped lower in the sky, nighttime approaching. But what night it was, she couldn't even venture. No one had come back. She was alone in the room with only the photos that made her ill and grungy blanket and pillow. She gathered up the pictures that lay scattered across the ground and arranged them into a pile, facedown. She couldn't even look at them. It sickened her to know someone had been watching her and Christopher on the beach. That moment had been special, sacred—between only the two of them.

The slimy man from earlier would come back for her—that wasn't a question. Maybe other men would be with him. And they needed her cooperation. She needed to buy time. Maybe even offer to work with them. Pretend she'd steal the information they needed. Find out if they were working in conjunction with Edwards. They wouldn't kill her if she could be an asset to them.

A chill snaked down her spine as she remembered the man's words from earlier: You're mine tonight. No way in hell was she going down without a fight. But how much fight did she have in her? She was exhausted, dehydrated, sick to her stomach. Could she really fight off a man twice her size in this condition?

A single tear slid down her cheek.

Where was Christopher?

***

The six men on Christopher's SEAL team gathered in the CO's office on base, looking down at the paper Brent tossed onto the table.

"You're sure this is it," Christopher demanded, looking at the numbers and letters in front of him.

"That's the plate," Brent said, "as well as the make and model of SUV. The police pulled it off the surveillance footage from the garage. They're coordinating an effort to pull up images from all the traffic cams in the area and surrounding businesses."

"Fuck no," Christopher said.

The eyes of every man on his SEAL team slid to him. His CO crossed his arms, waiting for an explanation. Patrick raised his eyebrows.

Adrenaline surged through Christopher. For the first time all evening they had a solid lead. A fucking chance. Hope bloomed in his chest, almost greater than the fear that had sat heavily there all afternoon. "That model SUV has built-in GPS navigation. We don't need traffic cams, we need access to the automaker's system. We can track the vehicle anywhere."

"For real?" Matthew asked, looking impressed.

"Hell yeah. That's why I was so angry earlier that they ditched Lexi's phone. We could've tracked her using that."

"What about her electronics?" Patrick asked. "Wasn't her computer stolen from her vehicle?"

"Already checked earlier. It's turned off. It's highly unlikely they'd bother shutting off the GPS in their vehicle though. Even if they weren't using it at the moment, it was running in the background. As soon as I find it in the system, we can follow every movement of the SUV, including where it is now."

"And it'll lead us straight to Lexi," Patrick finished.

Christopher looked at him, eyes grim. Patrick's cool blue eyes met his, and he nodded. Patrick knew what it was like to live in fear that the woman you loved might be harmed.

"She better be there. Because I'll kill those mother-fuckers myself."

The CO's eyes scanned over the SEAL team. "This is off the books. We have no legal authority to be doing the job of the police, running after Christopher's girl. If something goes wrong, I won't be able to help any of you. A move like this could be career-ending."

"The entire Atlantic fleet couldn't stop me," Christopher ground out.

"We'll handle this as a team," Patrick agreed, eyes blazing. "Lexi is one of ours now."

The other men all nodded and grunted in agreement.

"How long will it take to trace the vehicle?" Brent asked. His eyes blazed in anger.

"Minutes. Those systems are easy to hack into— minimal security compared to government databases like ours." He chuffed out a laugh, his first all day. Could it really be that damn easy to find her? He could only hope.

A few quick keystrokes, and he'd easily accessed the system. The movements of the SUV followed Lexi's exact path that afternoon. They'd been parked near base, followed her to the condo. Presumably they were the one's who'd broken the window on Lexi's vehicle. And when they hadn't found what they needed, they'd nabbed her.

"The vehicle's been in the same spot for two hours," Christopher said, his heart racing.

"That's where Lexi is," Patrick ascertained.

"We've fucking got 'em," Christopher confirmed.

The entire team moved instantly, rushing to gather their supplies. Ten minutes later the team was on the move. They exited base and minutes later flew over the bridge heading toward Norfolk. Christopher's gut clenched as he white-knuckled the steering wheel, his mind racing. Lexi was there—she had to be. But had she been harmed? Was she still alive? The alternative was unthinkable.

***

Lexi scrambled to her feet as she heard shouts. The overhead lights flickered several times, and then the room went black. Silence. The very last rays of the evening sun came in through the window, providing a dim glow in one small area of the confined room. In a few minutes, she'd be here in total darkness. Alone. Vulnerable.

Heavy footsteps resounded in the hall. She scrambled off to the corner of the room, trembling. Were the men fighting over what to do with her? Had something else happened? The doorknob jiggled and then she heard someone fumbling with the lock. Muffled voices. She raced over to the door, pressing herself flat against the wall beside it. The world seemed to sway. She shouldn't have moved so fast. The effects of the drugs they'd given her were slowly wearing off, but rushed movements made her dizzy.

If she could hide behind the large door when it swung open, maybe she could make a run for it. She'd only have a second, but in the dim light, she might just have a chance. They'd look first to the blanket and pillow. When they stepped into the room, she'd hurry out. How fast or how far she could go was uncertain.

A click, and then the heavy door swung open. She tensed, expecting the man from earlier. Several large men charged in, and she froze in fright. Was that…were those…?

She wanted to run but couldn't make herself move. Dizziness overtook her, and she started to stumble to the side. A large man ran to her, dressed in black, a mask covering his face. He hauled her up into his arms. "It's okay darlin'."

She'd heard that voice before.

Commotion ensued as someone else entered the room. The lights suddenly came back on, and Lexi squeezed her eyes shut. She heard a thump and saw a man on the ground, blood spilling from his chest. Lexi hadn't even heard a gunshot.

The man holding her yelled at the others.

"Tell Christopher we found her," one of them barked. "She needs medical attention."

The world faded to black.

***

"We found her," Brent's voice came through Christopher's ear bud. "Repeat, we found her." Christopher paused, mid-sweep of one of the upstairs bedrooms. His eyes continued a quick scan of the room, but he was literally frozen in place. "Mike's attending to her now, but she needs medical attention."

Fucking hell

That spurred him back to life. "Where are you?" Christopher demanded.

The team had split up upon arriving at the house, with Christopher, Evan, and Patrick going one way, the rest of the team another. Patrick appeared in the doorway and nodded at him as Brent gave their location down in the basement. Christopher tore down the stairs from the top level of the home, taking several at a time. Two men lay on the floor of living room, but he stepped over them, rushing to the second set of stairs. Racing to get his girl.

Matthew appeared holding Lexi. She was limp in his arms and so very pale. His chest clenched. What the hell had they done to her?

Brent appeared behind him, holding a stack of something in his hands. He shoved them at Christopher, saying he would destroy the remaining copies. Christopher didn't even glance down at the pictures. He took Lexi from Brent and rushed her outside as Mike called for an ambulance.

Her pulse was weak, and she was cold and pale, but he didn't see any external injuries. She was fully clothed, and Christopher nearly fell to his knees, grateful that she hadn't been harmed. He took her to his truck as sirens sounded in the distance. She'd be okay. They'd be okay.

His phone buzzed, and he pulled it from his pocket. His CO had texted the entire team: Edwards is in custody.

Christopher breathed a sigh of relief. Lexi mumbled something, and he swept his hand across her forehead, brushing her hair aside.

Violet eyes met his.

"Christopher," she murmured.

"I'm here, honey. Everything's all right."

Epilogue

Christopher carried Lexi down the hall to his apartment two days later, only setting her down to pull his keys from his pocket. He was half tempted to kick the damn door down, he was so eager to get her alone.

Lexi gazed at him through lowered lashes as she stood at his side. For just a moment, she was that shy, bashful girl again. And he was a big, tough, Navy SEAL, ready to show her the time of her life. Too bad one kiss from her a lifetime ago was all it had taken for him to fall head over heels. He'd never meant for them to be together more than one night, but after that first kiss in Coronado? He'd been hers. And after nearly losing her this week? He wasn't ever letting her go.

"All my stuff is at the hotel," she protested.

"Not exactly. Remember when Kenley stopped by the hospital to visit you last night?"

"Yeah…."

"I convinced her to bring your things here. She agreed it was for the best." He winked, knowing Lexi wouldn't like them deciding what to do without her input.

"For the best, huh? And how on Earth did you get her to agree to that?"

"She may have made me promise that I introduce her to some of the guys on my team," Christopher chuckled.

"Sounds about right," Lexi muttered. "I can't believe my best friend would betray me like that."

Christopher chuffed out a laugh. "I plan for us to spend all the time you're getting off from work together."

"Two weeks isn't bad considering everything I dealt with."

Christopher's eyes narrowed. Lexi had been joking about the situation, but it unnerved him. He'd thought he'd lost her, and hearing her treat it lightly didn't sit well. He wanted to protect her and care for her. Love her.

He unlocked the door, and they walked into his apartment together. She'd barely set her purse down, before he pulled her into his arms. She glanced up at him—so soft, so innocent, so damn perfect for him. "Lexi."

"Christopher."

"I was scared out of my mind that I lost you."

Her hands rose, and she cupped his face. "I was scared, too. But I'm okay, sweetie."

Sweetie.

That one little word was enough to nearly make him come undone.

"I can't stand the thought of not having you in my life, of spending another ten years, a lifetime, without you."

"We'll make it work," she said.

Hope bloomed in his chest. He was worried he'd have to convince her to give things a go. He clasped her hands, lowering them between them, and brushed a soft kiss over her lips.

"You're the only woman I've ever loved."

Shock filled her eyes.

"Honey, it was always you. No one but you…."

***

Lexi froze, her heart palpitating. Certainly he'd been with other women over the years. But had he truly only ever loved her? He bent and kissed her again, the rough stubble of his jaw chafing against her skin as his hot lips moved over her.

Christopher abruptly stopped and took a step back from her, reaching into his pocket. "I want to do something I should've done years ago."

Confusion flooded through her, and her heartbeat sped up.

In an instant, he was down on one knee before her. Heat bloomed over her skin. Love filled her heart. "Marry me, Lexi," he said, his voice thick with emotion. "I want to spend the rest of my life loving you, making you the happiest woman in the world."

"But…when did you get that?"

"I bought it for you a lifetime ago. I was just a dumb kid, and I never should've let you walk out of my life. Losing you was the biggest mistake I've ever made, and loving you is the easiest thing I've ever done."

Tears slid down her cheeks, and he took her trembling hand in his own larger one.

"I couldn't get rid of it. Maybe, in the back of my mind, I always knew I'd find you again. That you were the only one for me."

"Yes," she whispered.

"Yes, you'll marry me?"

She beamed, her face wet with her tears. "Yes, I'll marry you, Christopher."

He slid the ring onto her finger, then rose, capturing her mouth in a kiss. She'd always been his, even if she didn't know it. And now it was finally time to start their own happily-ever-after.

Author's Note

Thanks for reading A SEAL'S SURRENDER! I loved writing Christopher and Lexi's story. Theirs was a second-chance romance for the ages. Christopher was her first love, first real boyfriend, first everything. When he left her a decade ago, she'd never really gotten over him. (And never really, ahem, been quite so happy with another man.) We'd also heard Christopher mention his ex in passing a few times to the rest of the SEAL team. What man still mentions an ex from that long ago unless he'd never really forgotten about her?

Lexi had moved on with her life with a fast-paced, successful career. Something was missing though—and when these two finally got together? It was an explosion!

I'd love to write their backstory someday about how they met and their time as a couple back in Coronado.

In the meantime, make sure to pick up the next

book in the series, A SEAL'S SEDUCTION, to read all about Mike and Kenley!

xoxo,

Makenna

About the Author

Makenna Jameison is a bestselling romance author. She writes military romance and romantic suspense with hot alpha males, steamy scenes, and happily-ever-afters.

Her debut series made it to #1 in Romance Short Stories on Amazon. Makenna loves the beach, strong coffee, red wine, and traveling. She lives in Washington DC with her husband and two daughters.

Visit www.makennajameison.com to discover your next great read.

Want to read more from
MAKENNA JAMEISON?

Keep reading for an exclusive excerpt from the fourth book in her Alpha SEALs series, *A SEAL'S SEDUCTION.*

Kenley Bristow has her future mapped out: she'll meet a nice guy, settle down and have kids, and live the stable family life that she never had growing up. The last thing she wants is the assertive Navy SEAL who pinned her against the door, his hard body filling hers with desire she'd never felt before.

Navy SEAL Mike "Patch" Hunter prefers his relationships to be only one night. The petite woman with the face of an angel wasn't who he thought she was. But after he felt her trembling beneath him, he knew one taste would never be enough.

When an accident leaves Kenley injured and alone, she's forced to call on the one man she swore she'd never see again. But with heat she's never felt before burning between them, can she fend him off long enough to escape what she really fears—a life together?

Chapter 1

Mike "Patch" Hunter locked and loaded his HK416 assault rifle, taking aim at the target downrange. There was a slight breeze on the brisk autumn day, whispering across his skin, and he adjusted his calculations accordingly. It was cool out. Clear. His finger itched as he caressed the trigger, ready to take the shot. Guaranteed to meet his mark. The target sat immobile 200 yards from where he stood, not exactly the same as the fast-moving targets his SEAL team took out in battle. But hell, he'd taken plenty of kill shots to unaware men. Drug kingpins. Terrorists. Armed guards. All part of his duty to Uncle Sam and the US Navy.

Just this spring his SEAL team had been sent on an op to the Middle East to retrieve a high-value asset. The other guys had been on the ground ready to grab him. Mike had the sniper's roost across the street, and when their target—needed captured not killed—stepped out of the building flanked by two bodyguards, he'd taken them out in an instant. Pow. Pow. They hadn't even known what had hit them.

Mike spat on the ground beside his dusty boots before returning his eyes to the prize. The men around him fired off shots on the range, and a couple of his SEAL buddies stood behind him, watching, but he tuned everything out. Let his vision tunnel. The only thing that existed was the target.

The slight chill in the air nipped at his skin. He blinked. Focused. It was nothing but him and his weapon. In the zone.

Eye on the scope, he pulled the trigger.

Bullseye.

Every damn time.

"Not bad, man," his fellow team member Christopher "Blade" Walters said as Mike pulled off his headset and glanced back. Christopher lounged beside Brent "Cobra" Rollins, both of them looking relaxed and ready to roll onto the next part of their Saturday.

Despite their intense training at Naval Amphibious Base Little Creek Monday through Friday, the three of them had headed to a local gun range today to get in some practice and unwind. Or something like that. What was it about weapons and fresh air that made a man so damn content? The adrenaline rush of his job was what kept Mike going half the time, ready to take on the whole world. And shooting on the weekend with his buddies? He was fired up and ready to go, energy surging through his veins.

"Not bad?" Mike laughed. "That was fucking spectacular."

Brent raised his eyebrows. "Modest as always,

asshole."

"I get it," Mike said. "You're jealous of my good looks, talent, and way with the ladies."

Brent guffawed. "Not a chance in hell."

Mike held back a grin. While some of the guys on their SEAL team were content playing happily-ever-after with their women, Mike, Brent, and the third single guy on their team, Matthew "Gator" Murphy, still enjoyed carousing for ladies at the local bar. Although Mike enjoyed female company when the mood struck, he usually kept things light. The chase was part of the fun, and some of those girls that hung around him and the other guys were just too damn easy to be caught.

While Mike and Matthew had enjoyed their fair share of women over the years—hell, maybe more than their fair share—no one seemed to have more fun than Brent. A new woman every night was his MO, and the trail of broken hearts in his wake was a mile long. At least.

"Speaking of the ladies," Christopher interrupted as he stood. "I told Lexi I'd be back soon. Are you about wrapped up here or do I have to hoof it back to my apartment?"

Mike chuffed out a laugh. That guy was whipped. "Is she bringing any of her friends to the party tonight?" he nonchalantly asked as he gathered his gear.

Christopher's gaze flicked over to him as Brent's ears perked up. "Kenley will be there, if that's what you're asking."

"Hell."

Brent guffawed. "She's still pissed at you?"

"Something like that," Mike muttered.

The petite, brunette beauty with a head full of curls and angelic face was a friend of Lexi's. Lexi and Christopher were old flames who had rekindled their love over the summer after a chance encounter. Lexi, an IT whiz, had been sent down to their base in Little Creek from the Pentagon to stop some attempted hackings to their secure networks.

When she was kidnapped by the man behind the ploy, her best friend Kenley had come racing to Virginia Beach to help find her. As Mike and Christopher had searched the condo Lexi had been in the afternoon she went missing, Kenley had appeared from one of the bedrooms. Mistaking her for an intruder, Mike had instantly pinned her to the wall. And holy hell.

Trapping her small, curvy frame against his had made him harder than steel.

At that moment, he hadn't even cared if she was the enemy or not. He'd had a sample, and he needed more.

Her soft breasts had pressed against his hard chest, her lips almost brushing against his neck as he held her in place, her soft breath whispering against his skin. His fingers had wound round both of her slender wrists, holding her immobile, and the vanilla scent she wore had permeated the room, making his mind fuzzy and his dick stand at attention.

The second he'd realized she was Lexi's friend, not a foe, he'd been a goner. He had images of holding her body against the wall every night as he drilled into her, sinking his throbbing cock into her soft, wet heat as she whimpered for more. As he pleasured her again and again. No doubt a woman as gorgeous as her was used to a man's attention, but hell if he wouldn't love to be the one to have the honor of exploring every one of her curves—and then making her come in every way imaginable.

She was so small, he could easily hold her up as he took her, lifting her petite body up and down his shaft. Her legs would wrap round his waist, and she'd arch back in ecstasy as he made her come in his arms.

On his cock.

He wondered if she tasted of vanilla or something else sinfully sweet. If she'd been wet as he held her there against his hard body—God knows he'd been thick and throbbing for her the second he'd touched her.

Not that she'd exactly seen it the same way.

She'd trembled for him, but from fear, not arousal. Christopher had growled at him to get off of her, and the split second he'd realized she was Lexi's friend, he'd gone from aggressor to protector. He'd wanted to haul her against him again, but this time, to keep her safe from the evils that were out there. From the men who'd kidnapped her best friend.

Something didn't sit right with him at leaving her alone and defenseless in her condo while he and Christopher continued their search for Lexi, but what choice had they had? Kenley was a grown woman; she wasn't his. If she wanted to stay there, they sure the hell couldn't stop her. And Lexi had been the one being held by a crazed kidnapper, the one who needed their help.

The memories washed over him as Brent smirked. "Time to make a move, lover boy. Send her flowers or some shit like that."

Mike raised his eyebrows. Brent had never bought a woman flowers in his life. He'd probably never taken a woman out on an actual date—his bed seemed to work just fine.

"She's still pissed as hell at you from what Lexi says," Christopher said, falling in step beside them as they walked off the range. "She didn't take you pinning her against the wall like some criminal too well."

"Don't I know it," Mike admitted.

"She asked about you though," Christopher added.

Mike swung his gaze over to his friend. The way his heart pounded in his chest like a damn freight train was annoying. So what if she asked about him. Didn't mean a fucking thing.

"I think she was hoping you got shipped out—without the rest of the team," Christopher laughed.

"Crash and burn, lover boy," Brent said.

"Damn it," Mike muttered. So much for making amends. She'd probably be perfectly happy never seeing him again.

"What's this chick look like anyway?" Brent asked, eyes sparking with interest.

"Don't ask," Mike and Christopher said in unison.

Hell, Mike could understand why Kenley would be mad at him. She'd trembled against the wall as his much larger body caged her in, and it sure the hell hadn't been with desire. She had to know why they'd be on her in an instant though. Everyone had been on edge the minute Lexi was taken. Kenley herself had raced down to Virginia Beach from DC in search of her best friend. It wasn't like he made a habit of grabbing defenseless women in their own homes. The condo had been the last known location Lexi had been, and when she'd appeared unexpectedly out of the bedroom, his training had kicked in instantly.

Mike and all of the guys on his SEAL team were trained to be alert and aware in all situations. To neutralize the threat, getting in and out with their asses in one piece. They worked seamlessly as one unit, and he and Christopher hadn't even needed to utter a single word to one another as they swept the condo.

The fact that Kenley had been on the receiving end of it had been unfortunate, but it's not liked he'd harmed her. Just held her in place until he could determine who she was—and desired her more strongly than he'd ever wanted a woman before. Must be that forbidden fruit thing—he shouldn't have her, so he wanted her that much more. Mike shook his head, clearing the heated images that had been burned on his brain.

The men walked out to the parking lot, stashing their gear in the back of Mike's large SUV. He slammed the trunk shut as they each climbed into the vehicle. "So Patch, what are you up to tonight?" Brent asked Mike, addressing him by his nickname. "I know Christopher's all pussy-whipped and busy with his woman."

"Sonofabitch," Christopher muttered under his breath.

Mike smirked. Despite Brent's ribbing, Christopher was happier than ever, engaged to the love of his life. If he wanted that, then awesome for him. Mike was content living alone, flirting with the pretty girls whenever he felt like it, spending the night with one every so often. He didn't mind doing the flowers and dinner song and dance some of the time as long as the woman he was with understood he wasn't after anything long term.

He really did need to talk to Kenley tonight and formally apologize. If one of his SEAL buddies was marrying Kenley's best friend, their paths would no doubt continue to cross from time-to-time. He didn't need her feeling uncomfortable around him, and if smoothing the waters between them led to anything more, well, he sure the hell wouldn't complain. Not when the memories of her lush little body pressed firmly against his filled his brain every night.

"We've got that bonfire on the beach tonight," Christopher said. "Didn't Patrick and Rebecca invite you?"

"Hell, I guess so," Brent muttered. "I need some female companionship though, not a night with you motherfuckers."

"Are you hitting up Anchors instead?" Mike asked as he started the engine.

Anchors, a popular bar in Virginia Beach, was usually packed with single military men and plenty of available women. Their team went there on the weekends, enjoying a few drinks with their buddies before taking a woman home for the night.

Their team leader Patrick "Ice" Foster and his girlfriend, Rebecca, had organized a get together on the beach tonight instead. Each single parents, they'd started dating last spring and been inseparable ever since. There'd been a brief stalking incident, when the spouse of one of Rebecca's clients had been following her, but all's well that ends well. That dude was in jail and his teammate, "Ice," who everyone thought would never date again, seemed smitten with his woman.

The couple had organized the beach bonfire tonight for the guys on the SEAL team and their dates. Mike supposed the women his teammates were dating didn't enjoy hanging around the loud, crazy pick-up joint. Not that he blamed them. If he did ever settle down, he sure the hell wouldn't be spending his weekends at Anchors. Not that he was exactly the settling down kind. Playing the field had suited him just damn fine. And with his career of frequent deployments, long days of training, and weeks or months away, that was probably for the best.

"That depends on who's going to be at this beach party," Brent said.

"Alison is bringing along some of her nurse friends from the hospital," Christopher said, smirking. Alison, a pediatric nurse, was Evan "Flip" Jenkins's girlfriend. She'd been promising to set up some of the single guys with her friends. Mike had taken one of the pretty nurses out on a date, but the way she'd thrown herself at him had been entirely unappealing. Even for a guy like him, used to having his pick of women, he enjoyed a little bit of a challenge. An easy lay wasn't exactly what he was after.

"Just steer clear of Kenley," Christopher added, his eyes sweeping toward Mike.

Mike gripped the steering wheel tighter. "How's that?" He swallowed, trying to ignore the feelings of lust and desire churning inside him at the mere mention of her name. Hell, the way the woman wound him up like that was unnerving.

"She's still madder than hell at you. Lexi only got her to agree to come by promising to keep you away from her."

"What's she still doing in town anyway?"

Kenley lived in Northern Virginia, near Lexi. After Lexi and Christopher had gotten engaged over the summer, Lexi had put in a job application to work on base here at Little Creek. She and Christopher had been together out in Coronado years ago, and if all went according to plan, they'd be working on the same naval base again before the year was up. Lexi could keep a position with the Department of Defense but live down here with Christopher. Since Little Creek's own head of network security had been arrested as part of the hacking scandal, a position was open. With her connections and computer expertise, she'd probably be a shoo-in.

That didn't explain why Kenley had stuck around all this time. He'd seen her once since their encounter at the condo, and it hadn't exactly gone well. She'd been fuming at him, and that petite little woman telling him off had gotten him harder than steel. Something about knowing that she didn't want anything to do with him made him want her all that much more. He was so used to women throwing themselves at him that he didn't know what to make of her hostility—that and the fact that he'd held her against him, yet never gotten a taste of those sweet lips. Usually when a woman was that close, it ended very differently.

Imagining scenarios of him pinning her down and kissing her senseless had kept him up night after night ever since their first encounter at the condo. Even going home with a woman from Anchors hadn't fully slaked his need. She'd provided a temporary distraction from the woman he really wanted—Kenley. He was dying to peel off her clothes—not to mention peel away the layers of armor she'd put up. Not that she'd fucking give him the time of day right now, let alone a damn chance.

There wasn't much reason for her to stay in town though now that everything had died down. Lexi was readjusting after her kidnapping and had Christopher. Maybe Kenley just needed a vacation—her parents did own that condo by the beach he and Christopher had found her in. Still, it had been several weeks since the entire incident. One of these days he fully expected her to head back home. Lexi would, too, at least temporarily until her new assignment hopefully came.

"I'm not sure. Lexi's trying to talk her into moving down here, too. How crazy is that?"

"I thought she worked at the Pentagon?"

"Defense contractor in Arlington. It's a big company; I think they have plenty of contracts down here."

"Perfect," Mike muttered.

"We need to lock you two in an empty room. No, scratch that—a room with nothing but a bed. Let you fuck it out," Brent laughed.

"Jesus," Christopher groaned. "I know she wants you to stay away from her, but can't you at least try to make amends or something? Lexi and I are going to be planning a wedding soon. I don't want Lexi stressed out every time the two of you are in the same room."

"Yeah, yeah, I'm on it," Mike muttered. All he had to do was apologize to a petite, hotter-than-hell woman who loved to mouth off to him. What a freaking spectacular night this was going to turn out to be.

<u>Now Available in Paperback!</u>

37350270R00122

ROMANCE

He's the one man she can never forgive...or forget.

Lexi Mattingly, a hotshot Pentagon security specialist, can't escape her past. Sent down to Little Creek to track down hackers attempting to infiltrate Top Secret naval databases, the last man she expects to run into is the ruggedly handsome Navy SEAL she left in Coronado a lifetime ago.

Navy SEAL Christopher "Blade" Walters has carried a torch for a decade. The sparks ignited years ago on the beaches of California never burned out, and the man destined to be alone feels them slowly combust when the woman he'd lost forever walks back into his life.

Lexi and Christopher must learn to work together to stop the hackers. But when she's kidnapped from her hotel, Christopher may be the only man who can save her. Can she trust the man who broke her heart to protect her life? And more importantly, can he convince her to give their love a second chance?

A SEAL's Surrender, a stand-alone novel, is book three in the addictive Alpha SEALs series.

ISBN 9781717911377

90000

9 781717 911377

WWW.MAKENNAJAMEISON.COM

HOW TO WRITE A PhD IN LESS THAN 3 YEARS

A PRACTICAL GUIDE

STEVEN HARRISON